THE TROUBLE WITH MAX

THE TROUBLE WITH MAX

PATRICIA H. RUSHFORD

MOODY PUBLISHERS
CHICAGO

Cover Design: Studio Gearbox.com
Cover Photography: Steve Gardner / PixelWorks Studio
Interior Design: DesignWorks Group (thedesignworksgroup.com)
Editor: Cheryl Dunlop

ISBN-13: 978-0-8024-6253-4

We hope you enjoy this book from Moody Publishers. Our goal is to provide
high-quality, thought-provoking books and products that connect truth to your
real needs and challenges. For more information on other books and products
written and produced from a biblical perspective, write to:

Moody Publishers
820 N. LaSalle Boulevard
Chicago, IL 60610

Printed in the United States of America

*To Lauraine Snelling and
Ruby McDonald, my first
critique partners and my
forever friends.*

AUTHOR NOTE

It may seem strange to some that I would choose heroes like Jessie Miller and Max Hunter—one with leukemia and the other living with an abusive aunt and uncle. I suppose it's because I have cared for children who have suffered and even died with life-threatening illnesses and have worked with children tormented with emotional and physical pain at the hands of abusive adults.

These children were so often brave and resilient and able to overcome great adversity. They showed me what being a hero is all about. As a pediatric nurse and then a counselor, I have always had a heart for children and a desire to help them in any way I can. My earlier nonfiction books *Have you Hugged Your Teenager Today?* and *What Kids Need Most in a Mom,* were written to help and encourage parents in their endeavor to better care for their children. *It Shouldn't Hurt to be a Kid* helps parents, teachers, and caregivers to recognize abuse and to help bring healing to broken children.

Several years ago, I began writing *The Jennie McGrady Mysteries* for kids because I love a good mystery and according to the fan mail I receive, so do kids. My goal has been to provide great, exciting, and adventurous stories, but also to empower kids to rise above the problems they may encounter in life. Jessie and Max do this very well. I hope my readers and fans will enjoy their adventures as much as I have enjoyed writing them.

With Love, Patricia Rushford
www.patriciarushford.com

CHAPTER ONE

"Look at those guys, Jess." Max skidded to a stop, and I almost piled into her.

"What?" I managed to stop my bike and get off. The guys she was talking about were half a block away. I cringed. One had an open leather vest that revealed a tattoo. He had biceps the size of watermelons. Definitely not the kind of person you'd want to meet in a dark alley. The tall, skinny one was smoking a cigarette, his face scrunched up like he was in pain.

"Can you believe it?" she said through gritted teeth. "Dealing drugs right here in the open—in a public park. Let's get them."

I'd never seen her that upset before, and it scared me. "C'mon, Max. We need to get out of here." My heart was thumping faster than a rabbit running from a fox. We'd been riding our bikes and had taken a shortcut through Centennial Park. I was ready to go home for more reasons than one. "M-maybe it's not drugs. Maybe they're just . . ."

"Yeah, right. I can spot a druggie a mile away."

I frowned, wondering how she could tell, but thought it best not to ask. "We should call the police." I turned my bike toward home.

"Quit being such a girl."

"I am a girl."

"Shh." Max held a finger to her lips. "They'll hear us."

"But . . ."

"Relax, Jess. They don't know we're onto them. We'll just get the proof we need on my camera and turn them in to the police. No problem." Max dug into her backpack and brought the camera to her face. She snapped a couple of pictures and dropped the camera back into her pack.

Not a problem for her maybe, but I, being the practical type, wanted to turn these characters over to the police the minute we saw them make the drug deal. Not Max. Max was the kind of person who'd run straight into an icy lake. Even in a heated pool I had to edge in an inch at a time.

"They're getting away." She leaned her bike against a maple tree. "Let's follow them."

"No. Let's report them to the police." I dropped the kickstand on my own bike and settled it next to Max's, still hoping to talk her out of going after the men.

"Humph. The cops will never believe us," Max insisted. "We need hard evidence."

I tried to hold her back, but keeping Max from doing something she'd set her mind on was like trying to hold back the Chenoa River during our rainy season. So, I did the only thing I could—I followed *her* while she followed them into an old fishing cannery by the docks. We ducked inside the dilapidated building and scrunched down behind barrels and boxes as we crept toward the voices. When Max finally stopped, I hunkered down, squeezed my eyes shut, and prayed we'd make it out of the place alive.

"I can barely hear them." Max nudged me. "We need to get a little closer."

I gulped back the hysteria clogging my throat. "No, we don't. Please, Max, let's go home."

My pleading ended when I heard a shuffle behind me and felt a heavy hand come down on my shoulder.

CHAPTER TWO

I knew the day we met that Max Hunter would be trouble. What I didn't know was that her troubles would also become mine.

I'm not sure why, but I liked Max from the minute I saw her, looking all wild and freaky in her baggy clothes and crazy hairdo. Max isn't at all like me, but we have two things in common. One, the other kids steer clear of both of us. It isn't because they don't like us, exactly. I think they're afraid of us, but for different reasons. And, two, we're both fairly new to the school. Max had just moved into the neighborhood. I've lived in the town of Chenoa Lake my entire life, but had been homeschooled until this year.

Max started coming to our school right after the holidays. I'd already been there for four miserable months. Max Hunter walked into the classroom the day we returned from Christmas break and everyone, including me, turned and stared. She wore baggy army-green pants with about ten pockets, and a long-sleeved red flannel shirt over a black tank top. I guess the style could have been grunge, but to me it looked more like thrift-store-reject. What stood out most about Max was her hair. That day she was wearing it spiked with colored stripes of maroon, black, and pink.

Her don't-mess-with-me gaze drifted over the room, settling on each of the twelve sixth-graders as though daring them to say or do anything that might show disapproval. No one did. She looked at me last, probably because I was farthest back where people were least likely to notice me. Her gaze fastened on me and stayed longer than it had on the others—like she was checking me out. Her look wasn't mean or even curious—just assessing. I caught something in her eyes that day—respect, maybe. I wasn't really sure.

Max kept to herself at first, like I usually did. Once in a while I'd catch her watching me. Or she'd catch me watching her. I'd smile at her, but she never smiled back. She didn't fit in any more than I did, but with Max it was like she didn't really want to. She was smart, and the two of us usually ended up with the highest test grades in our classes. And that was probably another reason the others didn't seem to want to hang around us.

Spring trickled in and our PE teacher decided it was time for softball. I dreaded having to play on a team, but didn't try to get out of it. Then one day an amazing thing happened. Max was great at sports, and she volunteered to be the captain of one of our teams. Her first responsibility was to pick her players. Out of all the kids in that sixth-grade PE class, Max picked me first, not last, like I usually am.

To say I was surprised would have been the understatement of the year. I'm not your usual sports type of person. I'm short and skinny with about as much muscle as overcooked asparagus. That comes on account of having had leukemia and being in chemotherapy since I was about six years old. I'm in remission now, which means the doctors can't find any cancer right now. But I could get worse at any time and maybe die. So when Max pointed at me, my jaw dropped and I just stood there.

Cooper Smally, the big guy standing next to me, whomped me on the shoulder and pushed me forward. "Get out there, dork."

It hurt in more ways than one when Cooper picked on me, which he often did. But for once I was grateful. He saved me from standing there like an idiot when I should have been loping to the other side of home plate to stand beside my new friend. At least I hoped she'd be my friend. I didn't have all that many. No surprise there. Having leukemia and a bald head makes a lot of people nervous. Mom says it's because they don't know what to say. Some people actually think they're going to catch the disease if they get too close. Some people are just weird.

Max put me on third base, and I did okay. At one point, a ball came right to me and I scooped it up. Of course, I fumbled but managed to keep the ball in the borrowed glove—which in itself was a miracle seeing as how my hand could have fit in it at least three times.

Anyway, I snatched the ball with my right hand and threw it as hard as I could to the first baseman, who happened to be Cooper Smally. The ball fell short and Cooper missed his chance to tag the hitter out. Cooper tore off his baseball cap and nearly stomped it into the ground. Then he came after me.

He pushed at my shoulders, which probably wouldn't have affected most kids, but being the weakling that I am, I stumbled backward and hit the ground with a *thud*.

That's when Max showed up. She yanked him up by the back of his shirt. "You pull something like that again, Cooper, and you're off my team."

Cooper's face was red and round as a beach ball, and I thought for a second he was going to cry. "You can't do that. Mr. Davis won't let you."

"I can do anything I want, Cooper *Smally*, and don't you forget it." She said his last name in a drawled-out way like she intended to make a point.

I cringed, not wanting the attention a fight would bring.

Cooper backed down then. I'd never have believed it if I hadn't seen it with my own eyes. He backed down to Max, who was not only a girl, but about half his size. Actually, they were close to the same height—Cooper was just big all the way around.

Right then and there, whether she deemed herself my friend or not, Max was my hero.

Mr. Davis looked up from his papers and shouted from the bleachers. "What's going on out there?" He must not have been paying much attention or he would have known.

Max glanced at him, then at Cooper. "Nothing, sir. Just a misunderstanding." She looked down at me. "You okay, Jess?"

"Yeah." I rolled onto my stomach and wiped tears from my eyes, hoping she hadn't noticed. When I got to my knees, Max held out her hand to help me up. I took it, glad for the assistance, because to tell the truth, I'm not sure I could have made it up on my own. "Good catch, by the way." Max grinned at me, then went back to her place on the pitcher's mound.

I dusted off my clothes and then went back to my position.

Three outs later, no thanks to me, I walked with the others to the batter's cage. I couldn't hit the ball any better than I could throw it, but that didn't seem to matter to Max. I struck out and she cheered me on like she did the others. We won the game—I should say Max won the game for us. Her pitching and batting were far superior to anyone—even Cooper.

I never did find out why Cooper was so mad at me. Guess it could have been because the ball only went about twenty feet when I threw it to him, but that was a pretty good throw for me.

My parents tell me that winning isn't everything so it doesn't matter if you're great at the game or not. What matters is that you do your best and have fun. Mr. Davis apparently agrees, because he gave me an excellent score for sportsmanship. I guess Cooper never got that message. Max did, though, and I loved her for it.

From that day on, Max and I have been friends. At first I didn't understand why she'd want to hang out with me. I'm not the most fun person to be around. For a while I thought maybe she felt sorry for me. I asked her about it one time and she laughed. "You really think that?"

"Well," I said, "I can't think of any other reason you'd want to be my friend."

"You're nice, Jessie Miller," she said. "You have the qualities I like in a person. And you've never once, not even when I first came to school, treated me like I don't belong."

I could have said the same about Max. She never looked at me like the others did—like I was some sort of space alien. Not that I blamed people for thinking that. I really do look a lot like the Asgard on *Stargate*—small, skinny, big eyes, and a bald head. About the only difference is that I don't run around naked.

I was surprised by her answer though—about being treated like she didn't belong. I'd always thought of Max as being the kind of person who didn't care what other kids thought. I liked hanging out with Max, except when she got into her adventurous mode. Like now.

So anyway, here we were, in this dark warehouse, inching forward so Max could get a closer look at the bad guys. Then I felt this heavy hand on my shoulder and I thought, *Uh-oh, we're dead.* My heart jumped into my throat. I whipped around.

The guy was huge and mean-looking in a friendly sort of way. He put a finger to his lips so I wouldn't yell. I looked from the gun in his hand to the sour look on his face. Max still hadn't seen him. She turned around about that time and started to scream. I put my hand over her mouth. She swatted my arm away and gave me a withering look, like I'd told on her or something.

I figured the guy was probably an undercover cop, so I relaxed a little. He hunkered down beside us and put a hand on each of our shoulders. "Listen close, kids. I want you to stay low and go outside. Get as far away from the building as you can."

"Why?" Max whispered.

"Because in about two minutes this place is going to be swarming with cops. And trust me—you don't want to be in the middle of it."

Max nodded. "They're drug dealers, aren't they? Jess and I saw them in the park downtown and followed them."

He sighed. "We'll talk about that later. Now go."

I wasn't about to argue. I grabbed Max's hand and turned around. My shoulder connected with one of the barrels and it clattered to the floor.

I froze. My heart stopped. Terror rolled over me like a tidal wave.

"What was that?" One of the bad guys raised a gun and looked our way.

The guy who'd warned us to get away swore under his breath and pulled us down. "Get on the floor and don't move." He brought his lapel mike close to his mouth. "Now!"

I didn't need to be told twice. I flattened out, my arms over my head and my cheek pressing into the cold concrete. The place smelled of gas and oil and grease and all the other putrid stuff you find in warehouses. Now I had another reason to worry. With my immune system being so weak, a place like this could be deadly. I tried not to think about all the germs flying into my nostrils or attaching themselves to my skin. Not that I had time to think too much about all that. The doors burst open and, like the guy said, the place was swarming with cops.

After all the shooting stopped, the big cop ushered us out of the building and over to a uniformed officer. "Kids, I'm Detective Allen Johnson. Officer Dean here is going to escort you to the police station."

"The police station?" I gasped. "You're going to arrest us?"

"I should." Detective Johnson gave us a smoldering look.

"On what charge?" Max started talking in this weird tough-guy accent—like the mobsters in the *Godfather* movies. "You got nothin' on us."

"How about obstructing justice for starters?" Despite his anger, I saw the corner of his mouth twitch as though he was trying not to smile.

"You want me to put them in a holding cell, Detective?" Officer Dean grabbed our arms and led us over to his squad car.

Detective Johnson set his hands on his hips. "Not yet. Just have them wait in my office."

"Okay, kids, get in the backseat." Officer Dean opened the back door. "Better cooperate or I'll have to cuff you."

"So cuff me." Max held out her arms in front of her like it was all some kind of game.

I sort of thought the officer was joking, but I wasn't about to call his bluff. I scrambled into the backseat and scooted to the far side, leaving plenty of room for Max.

"Just get in." Officer Dean was getting annoyed.

"Come on, Max," I pleaded. "Quit fooling around."

Max lowered her arms and climbed in beside me. "I've never worn handcuffs before. I wanted to see what it was like."

I rolled my eyes.

"Relax, Jess. We're not in any kind of trouble. They'll just get our statements and release us."

"They'll call our parents. My mom and dad will freak out." I didn't tell her what I feared most—that my parents would tell me

I couldn't hang out with Max anymore. Mom was already paranoid about our friendship. Max was too active and a little too adventuresome to suit her. Fortunately, my father wanted me to live as normal a life as possible despite the cancer. Not that I consider having Max as a friend *normal*.

Max frowned. "They won't need to call anyone." Under her breath she said, "I hope." For the first time since our crazy adventure started, Max actually looked worried.

As Officer Dean pulled away from the docks, I twisted around in my seat and looked back. The tall, skinny guy, the one we'd seen dealing drugs in the park, captured my gaze. His cold hard stare sent shivers up my back and gave me goose bumps. Maybe I'd watched too many cop shows, but I had the feeling the man would kill me if he ever got me alone. I turned around, hoping he stayed in jail for a very long time.

We waited about an hour for Detective Johnson, who eventually took our statements before lecturing us about the dangers of playing detective. "You kids could have been killed in there. The guns we use are real."

"We were only trying to help," Max said. "We didn't know you were already on to them."

"Well, we were, and you kids nearly messed up the bust." His gaze softened as he looked at my bald head and then met my eyes. "You're Jessie Miller."

I nodded and looked away.

"I know your father. Um—should you be . . . ?"

"I'm in remission," I blurted out. Sometimes it seems like everybody in town knows who I am. It's pretty hard to hide when you're like the town's poster child. A lot of people have donated money to help our family pay for my medical bills.

"Well, just the same, I think you need to be careful." He picked up his pen. "Now if you would give me your phone numbers, I'll call your parents to pick you up."

"No." Max shook her head. "Please don't call. They're not home anyway. Our bikes are right down the street in the park."

Detective Johnson looked from Max to me and then back again, suspicion glinting in his blue-green eyes.

"Please." I had never seen this side of Max. She looked really scared, and I wondered why.

"All right," he finally said. "I'll let you go, but from now on, no playing cops and robbers, okay?"

"Okay," I said.

Max didn't make any promises, and that worried me.

"If you ever see anything suspicious like that again, you give me a call. Don't try to gather evidence. That's our job." He handed each of us a business card. "Can you do that?"

"Sure." Max smiled up at him. "We'll get out of your hair so you can process those guys."

"They will go to jail, won't they?" I shifted from one foot to the other.

"Depends."

"On what?" I thought about the glaring look the drug dealer

had given me, and a shiver shot through me again.

"On what we can pin on them, for one thing," Johnson said. "Their past records for another." He must have read the fear on my face because he added, "You don't have to worry, though. Most of them are repeat offenders, so I doubt they'll get out anytime soon."

I wasn't completely convinced. I knew that if the guy didn't have any previous arrests, he could post bail and be out on the streets tomorrow. I also knew about the recent trouble the local police had been having with drug dealers—especially with meth. My parents had been talking about how easy it was for drugs to be brought into rural areas like ours. Worse than that, some people made their own.

I was glad the cops caught these drug dealers, but I was also worried that there were a lot of others out there. Worried about what Max planned to do about it, I also wondered why she felt she had to do anything.

We got to my house around two thirty in the afternoon. After I gave my mom a quick hug, Max and I went straight up to my room to debrief. That's what Max called it. Debriefing. Like when you talk about what happened after an upsetting experience.

Personally, I wanted to close my eyes and take a nap. The ordeal had physically exhausted me, but my mind was still reeling. I knew one thing—I would not be telling my parents about our little adventure, and I hoped Detective Johnson wouldn't either. They might decide I couldn't hang out with Max anymore, and I didn't think I could stand that.

Max flopped down on my bed and looked up at the constellation of glow-in-the-dark stars on my ceiling for a while. They weren't exactly glowing at the moment, but you could tell what they were. All of a sudden she jumped up. "We need closure."

I wasn't exactly sure what *closure* meant, but the sudden light in her eyes made me wonder if I shouldn't try to talk her out of whatever she had planned.

"Come on, Jess." Max jerked open my bedroom door and headed for the stairs.

"Where are we going?" I hated that question, because with Max I always seemed to be asking it.

"You'll see."

I hated her answer even more. Actually, *hate* is too strong a word. Part of me always holds back, afraid of what might come next. Another part of me looks forward to whatever excitement lies ahead. One thing was for sure—having Max for a friend was never dull. I followed her down the stairs and out the front door.

"Where are you going?" Mom came to the front door as we were getting on our bikes.

"Not to worry, Mrs. Miller. We'll just be downtown."

"Are you sure you're up to the ride, Jessie?" She tipped her head to the side, looking me over.

"I'm okay. I'll take a nap when I get home."

"All right." She had that I'm-not-sure-I-believe-you look. "Be back before dinner."

"I will."

"Be careful," she called after us. "And Jessie, call me if you need a ride home."

We got on our bikes and rode into town. We ride bikes a lot, actually. It's the best way to get around since there are wide bike lanes on most of the streets in Chenoa Lake. We live in a tourist town on a huge lake.

Our town isn't very big, and it only takes about five minutes to ride from one welcome sign to the other. It's one of those lake-side communities that have more tourists than residents—at least during the summer. Thousands of tourists come to visit every year.

The town sits on the banks of Chenoa Lake in the Cascade Mountains. In fact, the town and the lake have the same name. Max actually lives in Lakeside, which begins where Chenoa Lake ends. There's another town to the north called Hidden Springs. The three small towns share a courthouse, fire department, and police department, as well as a school, Lakeview, which has grades kindergarten through 12.

Max and I rode through downtown, which consists mostly of tourist shops all decorated on the outside to make the town look like an alpine village. There are art galleries and antique stores, clothing stores and little markets, T-shirt shops and a couple of candy stores, and restaurants. Lots of restaurants. Max put on her brakes in front of the Alpine Tea and Candy Shoppe and jumped off her bike.

"This is where we're going for closure?" I relaxed a little.

"Yep." Max grinned. Her smile is a little crooked, but I figured that's because her teeth are. She probably could benefit from braces, but I doubt her family has the money. Besides, her teeth are part of her quirky personality. There's a small gap between her two front teeth, which I think matches the gap in her brain on those times when she drags us into dangerous situations. Like the time she wanted to take a raft up to Miller Creek and shoot the rapids. That might have been fun except for the waterfall.

We'd just had a ton of rain, and with the snow melting off the mountains, the water was more furious than I'd ever seen it. Maybe my brain has a bigger hole in it than hers, cause I actually went along with the idea. I thought she knew the river. I thought she'd been on it before.

Wrong on both counts. The rafting trip was fun at first. The current took us over swells and sent us twirling in the little whirlpools. Within a few minutes I could feel the icy water seeping into my jeans and realized the raft was taking on water.

"Where did you get this thing, Max?" I had asked her. "It's leaking."

"At the thrift shop. They told me they'd fixed the leak. We'll just have to scoop the water out with our hands."

I grumbled and bailed while she managed the oars. After a few minutes, my hands felt numb and had turned a sickly shade of grayish blue.

Then I heard it, the unmistakable roar of a waterfall. And believe me when I say this was no trickle. The water picked us up and shot us forward. We both saw the drop-off at the same time and screamed. Neither of us could hear the other over the roar. I put my hands in the water and used all the strength I had to steer us toward shore.

As you might imagine, our paddling did about as much good as trying to hold the ocean back with a stick. As the raft tipped over the edge, we could see the river bouncing along about a hundred yards below. Okay, maybe it was more like twenty feet, but at the time it seemed like a long way down.

I closed my eyes and grabbed for the oarlocks, but my hands connected with the raft's slippery sides. Then I felt nothing but air as the raft abandoned us. Max and I plummeted to what I felt certain would be our death. I imagined us hitting the rocks and thinking that this might not be such a bad way to die. Quick and simple, not like the slow excruciating way you die when you have cancer.

But, of course, we didn't die. We hit the water with the force of a cannonball. The falls tumbled us around like rocks in a rock tumbler and finally spit us out into this pool of clear, sparkling water. I hit the surface sputtering and gasping for air. Max came up a second later. The first words out of her mouth were, "Wow! That was awesome."

I swear she was ready to try it again. "Max," I grumbled, "I am wet and freezing cold and I am going home." I looked up at the cliffs on both sides of the river and mumbled, "If we can find a way out of here."

I'm not sure how we managed to climb out of that canyon that day, but we did. Then we had to hike another mile to get to the place where we had left our bikes.

Needless to say, my parents were not happy. They grounded me for a week. That's when Mom first started making noises about my selection of friends and activities. We were all surprised I didn't end up with pneumonia. Doctor Caldwell, my oncologist, said it was probably because my cell count was nearly normal, the sun was shining, and we didn't sit around to wait for help. By the time we got to our bikes, our clothes were nearly dry.

Max never said, but I suspected she got into a lot more trouble than I did. I saw bruises on her cheek and arm the next day, but she refused to tell me what had happened. "It's nothing, Jess," she'd said. "I got these from the fall."

I didn't believe her. That was the first inkling I had that something in her life was terribly wrong. No wonder she'd been afraid when Detective Johnson mentioned calling our parents. For Max's sake, I'm glad he didn't.

CHAPTER FOUR

When we stopped in front of the Alpine Tea and Candy Shoppe, it didn't look like Max was planning anything as dangerous as a raft trip for our closure. Still I couldn't help but wonder what she was up to. I lowered the kickstand on my bike and followed Max into the shop, figuring she wanted to buy some candy. Wrong.

"Good afternoon, girls," Mrs. Cavanaugh greeted us.

"Afternoon, ma'am." Max walked past the candy counter and headed straight for the tea room.

"Hi." I waved, and then hurried to catch up to my friend.

Max took a chair at a table in the corner by the window. The spot offered a great view of the lake and of the hanging baskets of flowers Mrs. Cavanaugh always planted come springtime.

I loved the tea room and sometimes came for tea with my mother. The Cavanaughs were neighbors, and their daughter, Ivy, used to be my friend. Susan Cavanaugh and my mother were friends. In fact, several of Mom's watercolor paintings were displayed on the walls of the shop.

The delicious scent of spices and fresh pastries made my

mouth water. Unfortunately, being here with Max made me nervous. Like I said, I never knew what to expect. And Max wasn't exactly your tea-for-two type of person.

"What can I get for you?" Ivy sidled up to the table. Though her voice was pleasant enough, her eyes told me she didn't want us there.

I glanced over at Max, hoping for a clue as to what we wanted. All I wanted at the moment was to get out of there. "We'll have one high tea for two, please." Max lifted her chin and spoke in a fake English accent.

Ivy rolled her eyes, and then looked at me as if to get my okay.

High tea, even though we shared it, would cost around $18, and all I had in my pocket was two dollars. *We can't afford that,* I started to say. Max's withering look stopped me.

"Which tea would you like?" Ivy clamped her lips together. It killed her to be nice to Max and me. I wondered if that's why Max came in—to torment the girl. Here in the shop, Ivy had no choice but to treat us with the same courtesy as she did the other customers.

"I'll have the lavender infused Lady Grey," Max told her in the same silly accent.

"Um—mint," I managed to say without laughing.

Once Ivy left, I leaned across the table. "What are you doing? I don't have enough money to pay for this."

"Relax, Jess. I'll take care of it."

"Right." I couldn't help wondering how. Maybe Max got an

allowance. We'd never really talked about money, but I knew she didn't have much. A lump formed in the pit of my stomach. Did she plan on skipping out without paying? No, I told myself. Max may be eccentric, but she isn't a crook.

Looking out the window, I spotted Cooper Smally across the street. He was sitting on a bench in front of the ice-cream store, licking a supersized cone and staring at us.

"Don't look now," I said, "but Cooper's watching us."

Max turned and stared back at him. "Not for long."

She was right. Max kept staring and Cooper lasted about two seconds before looking away. He looked sad and I felt sorry for him. I'd never seen him around other kids his age. And at school he seemed about as friendless as I had been before Max came along.

"I think he likes you," Max said.

I about choked on my water. "What?"

"Haven't you noticed? He's always hanging around."

"Must be you he likes, then, cause it sure isn't me." I couldn't believe she'd say something like that.

Cooper left the seat and walked down the street to the next bench. He looked back at us, then away again. Max couldn't see him and I didn't say anything. Let him look.

The tea came and I tried my best to enjoy it. I figured, worst-case scenario, I'd have to call my dad and have him post bail. Most likely, I could charge it and tell Mrs. Cavanaugh I'd pay it later.

Mrs. Cavanaugh brought a three-tiered silver tray. We feasted on cucumber and cream cheese, smoked salmon, and deviled ham sandwiches.

Max slathered butter, strawberry preserves, and Devonshire cream over her freshly baked scone and took a dainty bite. Her eyes closed in ecstasy. "Mmm. These are my favorite."

My heart did a little somersault seeing her enjoy the food so much. I usually tried not to think about Max's home life, but there had been times I wondered if she got enough food. I usually brought extra stuff in my lunch bag, and she always ate it. I asked her once and she told me everything was fine at home and that I worried too much. I knew she was lying, but there wasn't much I could do about it.

My favorite dessert was the chocolate-dipped strawberries. I traded Max her two berries for a tart and I ate all four of them. The strawberries were plump and ripe and red and juicy.

Worth going to jail for. The thought brought me up short. Mrs. Cavanaugh wouldn't call the police, would she? The thought of going down to the station twice in one day turned my stomach upside down.

When we'd finished our tea, Ivy brought the check. I held my breath as Max got to her feet, reached into the front pocket on her right thigh, and pulled out a wad of bills. She peeled off two tens. Stuffing the rest back in her pocket, she ambled over to the counter, paid the bill, and gave Ivy a two-dollar tip.

Still in shock, I followed Max out of the shop and over to our bikes. I figured we'd head back over to my place, but Max had other ideas. She straddled her bike and waited for me to get on mine.

"Where did you get all that money?" I probably shouldn't have mentioned it, but I really needed to know.

"Earned it," was all Max said.

"Oh." I wanted to ask how, but she shot me a warning look. "Where are we going?" I asked instead.

"*I* have things to do. *You* are going home to take a nap."

I stiffened. "I don't . . ."

"Don't argue. I promised your mother I wouldn't wear you out, and I've already done that."

"I don't need you to tell me whether or not I should take a nap." I was pouting like a little kid, but I didn't care.

"I'll see you later." She began pedaling in the opposite direction from where I lived.

"Where are you going?" I yelled after her, but she disappeared around a corner without a backward look.

"Fine," I growled. "Be that way." I wanted to follow her and find out what she was up to. Unfortunately, she was right. I did need to rest. I turned my bike around and saw that Cooper was heading in the same direction Max had taken. "See," I muttered under my breath, "he does like you." Either that or he wanted to get her alone so he could beat her up.

I thought about following so I could warn Max, but decided against it. She was tough enough to stand up to Cooper Smally.

And I was more than ready for a nap. I rode home, feeling lonely and angry and very tired.

I wish I could be normal, full of energy and able to run all day. I wish I didn't have to be sick so much. But wishing does nothing but make me miserable.

By the time I turned into our driveway, I'd gotten over my anger. Now I was just worried. Had Max really earned all that money? How? We were together almost every day. When would she have had time? And where was she going in such a hurry? Why couldn't she have taken me along?

And what about Cooper? Why was he following Max? Did she know he was behind her?

I parked my bike in the garage and went inside, trying to put the mysterious Max Hunter out of my head.

The house was empty as it usually was on sunny Saturday afternoons. I grabbed my pillow and multicolored quilt out of the basket near the sliding back door and went out on the deck. "Hey, Mom. I'm home."

Mom looked up at me and waved. She was sitting on a folding wooden chair on the lawn with her watercolors and easel. Her name is Amy, by the way. Amy Miller, interior decorator, artist, and full-time mom since they first found out about the leukemia. I feel bad that Mom had to put her career on hold so she could take care of me. Mom says she doesn't mind as long as she can paint once in a while. So, most weekends she sets up her easel while Sam, my little brother, and I go fishing with Dad. And on days when I have about as much energy as a cooked noodle, I lie on the swing and read or sleep.

That's where I headed now. I tossed down the pillow and curled up under the quilt so I could watch my family. Sam and Dad were out in the boat, fishing poles in hand. My dad's name is Daniel. He's an architect and designs houses here in Chenoa Lake and other places. He built our house. Maybe that's why it's so perfect. The house isn't a mansion like Ivy's house next door, but it's practical and not nearly as expensive as some of the places our neighbors own.

A peaceful feeling washed over me. I have a good life really—except for being sick. Like I said earlier, school isn't so great either. Up until this year, Mom homeschooled Sam and me. I liked that, but missed being around kids my own age. So now I'm a student at Lakeview. And that's good, I guess. I like my teachers and my classes. If I hadn't become a student there, I might not have met Max.

All in all, it's not such a bad thing. Most of the kids are nice enough, but none of them go out of their way to actually include me or Max in their already established cliques. Ivy used to come over and play sometimes before I got sick and lost all my hair. Cooper Smally is the only one who gets mean, and he hasn't tried anything since his run-in with Max on the baseball field.

Mom says Cooper is afraid of me—of the cancer. His mother had breast cancer and died last year. She lost all her hair too. Cooper acts like it's my fault. I feel bad being a constant reminder to him, but there isn't much I can do about it. Maybe someday I'll tell him so. I thought again about him looking at Max and me from across the street. The fact that he'd followed Max troubled me. I'd have to ask her about it tomorrow.

My mind drifted back to the other kids and school. You wouldn't think having hair could make such a huge difference in a person's life. For most people, hair grows back after chemo. It didn't for me. I tried wearing a wig for a while, but it was hot and itchy and it would slip off when I played. I also tried those pretty scarves, but they never stayed where they belonged. Now I wear caps and hats sometimes, but those make my head itch too.

Mom thinks I look cute bald and Sam likes rubbing my head. Dad says it gives me character. I smiled at the thought.

Not that it matters. This is the way I am now, and if the kids at school don't like it, tough. Max doesn't even seem to notice.

I inhaled a lungful of fresh mountain air, closed my eyes, and fell asleep.

After my nap I went into the bathroom to wash up. When I came out I heard voices in the kitchen.

"I'm glad Jessie invited you for dinner, Max," Mom was saying. "You're welcome in our home anytime." I thought it was cool that Mom and Dad would be so accepting of Max even though she wasn't the type of friend they would have picked for me. Maybe they were just happy that I finally had a friend. On the other hand, if they knew about the drug deal and how we almost got shot, that could change.

"Thank you, Mrs. Miller. Um—is Jessie around?"

"She should be down any minute." Mom set out five plates on the dining room table.

I came in and leaned against the wall, my arms folded. I was still ticked about her disappearing act earlier and wasn't sure what to think about the dinner invitation—especially since I hadn't invited her.

"We'll have to have your parents over for dinner soon." Mom smiled at her. "I'd love to meet them."

"My parents are dead."

Just like that. No tears, no looking away like it was hard to talk about. Had I heard her right? I pushed away from the wall and climbed up on the stool next to her at the kitchen counter. "I didn't know that."

"Why do you think I live with my aunt and uncle?"

I shrugged. "I never really thought about it." It made sense though—especially since she always referred to them by their first names. "What happened to them? Your parents, I mean."

"They died in an airplane crash when I was five. My dad was a private pilot, and they were coming back from a business trip." She reached over and took a carrot stick from the relish tray Mom had just taken out of the fridge. "They were flying up the coast and went down in the ocean near San Francisco."

"How awful." Mom placed a bowl of veggie dip in the center of the raw vegetables. "Have you been living with your aunt and uncle ever since?"

Max nodded. "Mostly."

I bit my lip and wondered if Mom had picked up on the sarcastic tone in Max's voice.

"What are their names?"

I could tell that Max was uncomfortable with the questions, but she answered anyway. "Bob and Serena Schultz."

"Serena . . ." Mom frowned. "Does she work at Jillian's Hair Palace?"

Max dropped her gaze to the counter. "Yeah. She likes to call herself a cosmetologist."

My mother definitely caught the sarcasm that time. She raised an eyebrow. "And your uncle?"

"He's a manager at the Hanson's grocery store in Lakeside."

It was time to rescue my friend. "Come on, Mom—enough with the 20 questions."

Mom laughed. "I'm sorry. I just like to know my children's friends."

I grabbed Max by the arm. "Let's go out on the deck until dinner's ready." I really wanted to get Max alone to ask some questions of my own, but that didn't happen. Dad and Sam were bringing the boat in.

"Hey, did you catch anything?" Max waved at the duo and jogged down the stairs, across the lawn, and onto the dock to help them tie up.

"We caught us some dinner." Sam held up a mess of trout. "You guys can help us clean 'em."

I wandered down the hill and watched Dad, Sam, and Max each take a fish, slice open the belly, scrape out the guts, and wash the fish before setting them in a plastic bucket.

Dad grinned over at Max as she grabbed another fish. "You handle those like a pro."

"My uncle used to work on a fishing boat. I went along sometimes." Max had a wistful expression, and this time there was no hint of sarcasm. "He let me catch fish as long as I cleaned them." I tucked the new information away with the other things I'd learned about Max.

An hour later the fish had been breaded and fried and they lay on a platter in the center of the dining room table. When Dad asked who wanted to say grace, Sam's hand shot up like it always did.

"All right, Sam." Dad chuckled, knowing what would come next.

My little brother is adorable, but totally predictable. Giving us all a sly look, his arms shot into the air and he began singing to the original theme from *Superman*. "Thank You God, for giving us food . . . Thank You God for giving us food. For the food that we eat, for the friends that we meet, thank You God for giving us food."

"That was totally cool, Sam." Max laughed so hard I thought she was going to slide to the floor. "I've never heard anybody pray like that before. My grandpa used to make us all bow our heads and be really quiet. Then he'd pray so long our food would get cold."

"Dad does that, too, sometimes," I teased. "But usually only at Christmas, Thanksgiving, and Easter."

Dad grinned. "My prayers aren't that long, and besides, it doesn't hurt to be formal once in a while."

Despite the good mood around the table and Sam regaling us with fish stories, Max seemed preoccupied and sad. We'd only been friends for about two months, but every day brought new concerns. Max was in trouble and I wanted to help her, only I had no idea how.

She decided to leave after we'd done the dishes.

"Are you mad at me or something?" I asked as I walked her out to the porch.

"No."

"Then what's the matter?"

Max sighed, glanced my way, and then looked down at her scuffed-up tennis shoes.

"Tell me. Maybe I can help."

Max didn't say anything for a minute. She pulled her ratty old jacket close around her. Then in the saddest tone I'd ever heard, she said, "You can't help, Jess. No one can."

She climbed on her bike and rode away.

CHAPTER FIVE

The next morning I called Max to invite her to Sunday school. I usually asked the day before, but had forgotten about it last night. She never came, but I figured I'd keep asking. Her phone rang six times before someone answered.

"Hello." The voice was gruff and angry, and I figured I'd awakened her uncle, and then I felt bad.

"Um—is Max there?"

"There's no one by that name living here. You got the wrong number." He must have slammed the receiver down cause it sounded like a gunshot. Well, almost. I checked the number Max had given me, and then looked in the phone book under Bob Schultz. It was the right number. How could I have had the wrong name?

I didn't say anything to Mom and Dad—just told them Max must have gone somewhere. We went to church in Lakeside, close to where Max lived. If she really lived there.

Our church had been built in 1923—at least that's what is written above the door. It has a carved tin ceiling and stained glass windows, a tall steeple, and a bell. The bell was ringing when we pulled into the parking lot. I looked around hoping maybe Max had decided to come. She hadn't.

Going inside always made me feel like we were on the set of *Little House on the Prairie*. Although the church had been remodeled, everything was like it had been when it was built. It was on the Historical Registry and one of the places tourists liked to go.

All through the service, I thought about Max, wondering what I should do or if I should do anything. She'd all but told me to butt out. Normally I would have, but Max is my friend and I was more convinced than ever that she needed help. She'd looked so sad the night before, and that wasn't like her. Max was funny and brave and crazy.

I took a nap after church so I wouldn't get too tired later. Sam and Dad went fishing, and Mom set up her watercolors and easel on the bank of the lake. She painted landscapes mostly, kind of like the French impressionist, Claude Monet—soft and delicate and easy to look at. In art class I had picked him to write a report on because his work reminded me of Mom's. She was saving up for an art show next month during the big art and music festival the town holds every year. I hope she sells a lot. We need the money for all my medical bills. That's something else I feel bad about. Sometimes I think it would be better for them if I just died.

I don't say things like that anymore. I did once last year and Mom cried. She and Dad both told me the money didn't matter. They wanted to do everything humanly possible to keep me healthy. They even told me I was their gift from God. I smiled at that. I don't see myself as much of a gift. One thing I know for sure, they love me.

I wondered again about Max. It would be horrible to lose your parents. Did Bob and Serena love her?

I woke up at two and told Mom I was going to ride my bike over to Max's. Usually on Sunday she calls or comes over. Mom waved at me and yelled, "Be careful and call if you need us to pick you up."

"I will."

I rode through town, looking for any sign of Max. I'd gotten her uncle's address out of the phone book and looked it up on the map. After riding for fifteen minutes, I pulled into the driveway of a single-story house in Lakeside. The development had gone in about five years ago, but was already starting to look dumpy.

"Please be here, Max," I mumbled as I got off my bike and started up the walk. I was almost to the door when I stopped. My stomach hurt with all the knots forming inside. I felt like I was about to get up in front of the entire school to give a speech. The man on the phone this morning had sounded angry. I didn't want to face him again. He'd already told me Max didn't live here, but she did.

Unless she'd been lying to me. Maybe Max was really homeless and had made up the stuff about her uncle and aunt.

I took a deep breath and stepped up to the door, raising my

hand to ring the doorbell. Loud, angry voices came from inside, so I lowered my arm and listened.

"Alice Hunter," a woman screamed. "You give me that money right now or I'll have your uncle beat the . . ."

"You gave it to me," someone else yelled back. Alice? It couldn't be. The voice definitely belonged to Max.

"You little liar. Why would I give you a hundred dollars? You stole it."

"I don't steal!"

I heard a *thunk*. "What's the use?" Max screamed back at her. "Here's your stupid money. It isn't worth getting beat up over."

Half a second later, the door flew open and Max nearly collided with me on her way out.

I jumped back, my mouth open, words stuck somewhere between shock and horror. Through the still-open door I could see a woman wearing a silky turquoise robe, her hair wilder than anything Max had come up with. She was standing in the middle of the messiest room I'd ever seen, a cigarette dangling from her lips.

Max grabbed the knob and pulled the door shut. "What are you doing here?"

Her anger swept over me like a thunderstorm.

"I . . . I came . . . I wanted . . ." Somehow the words wouldn't come. All I could think of was the scene I'd just heard and the flaming red spot on Max's cheek. "Oh, Max." Tears filled my eyes. I couldn't help it. "What happened to you?"

"Forget it. Just forget it. I mean it, Jess. If you tell anyone . . ." Max brushed past me and headed for her bike. She hopped on and pedaled like crazy. This time I went after her.

She was much faster than I, and I probably would have lost her if I hadn't caught sight of her every now and then along the curved road that followed the lake. She turned onto the road leading to the state park, and I spent the next half hour riding around the park looking for her. I finally spotted her bike off the trail leading to the falls, the very waterfall she and I had gone over on the rafting trip. I had this sick feeling in the pit of my stomach that she might hurt herself.

"Don't do anything stupid, Max," I muttered under my breath. I parked my bike next to hers and headed for the waterfall. I found her sitting on a rock, staring down at the water. Without saying anything I climbed up beside her.

After a while she looked over at me. "I wish you hadn't seen that, Jess. Now I'm going to have to kill you."

CHAPTER SIX

I blinked several times. Had I heard her right? She was going to kill me?

"Gotcha." She chuckled.

"Max Hunter. That's a terrible thing to say." I laughed despite my determination not to.

"Well, you shouldn't have come to my house."

"I was worried about you. I called this morning, and the guy who answered said you weren't there." I frowned. "Actually he said Max didn't live there. But your name isn't really Max, is it?"

"Max was my nickname when Mom and Dad were alive. My middle name is Maxine." She stretched out and rolled over onto her stomach, head facing the falls. "After they died, I made everyone call me by my real name, Alice."

"But you told everyone at school your name was Max."

She closed her eyes and rested her head on her arms. "I know. I'm not sure why I did that. Maybe because I wanted to be Max again. Max was happy and . . ." She turned away from me. "It's stupid. Forget I said anything."

"I can't forget that, and I can't forget what Serena did to you. She hit you, Max. She left a bruise. And it's not the first time. That's child abuse. You need to tell someone."

"No!" She stood up so fast I thought she was going to fall off the cliff. "And you'd better not say anything either. Besides, I'm not a child."

"But you can't let them hurt you like that." I got up and put my hands on my hips. I'd never confronted Max before. When she reached for me, I thought for sure she was going to push me over the edge.

"Look, Jess." Max placed her hands on my bony shoulders like I was a little kid and she, the adult. "I know you want to help, but it's not as bad as it looks. Serena just woke up and she—well, she's not in the best mood in the morning. I shouldn't have argued with her."

"She shouldn't have slapped you."

Max climbed off the rock and started down the trail. "She didn't mean to hurt me."

"But in a foster home you wouldn't . . ."

"What, get slapped around? Boy, are you wrong about that. When my mom and dad died, I got sent to a foster home. My foster parents locked me in the closet and left me there for hours. Bob and Serena found out and took me in. They didn't know how to raise a kid, and they hadn't been married very long. They're doing the best they can."

"But you said you were only five. How can you remember?"

"Uncle Bob has told me lots of times."

As a threat, I thought. "Most foster parents aren't like that," I said instead.

"How would you know?"

"I'm sorry you had a bad experience with foster care. But your aunt and uncle are abusing you too. Why are you making excuses for them?"

"I'm just telling you how it is, okay?"

I didn't say anything. When Max decided to do something, nothing short of a natural disaster could change her mind.

"As long as I stay out of their way, things are okay." She stuffed her hands into the pockets of her jacket. "I can take care of myself."

"They do drugs."

She stopped and I almost ran into her. Max swung around, her eyes flashing. For a second, I thought she might hit me. "Who told you that?"

"N-nobody. I can tell. We have those movies at school and I saw . . ."

"You saw nothing." Max raised her fist. "You got that?"

I swallowed hard and nodded.

She dropped her arms to her side. "You gotta promise me you won't tell anyone."

"But . . ."

"I mean it, Jess." She started walking again. "I consider you my friend, and I'm gonna give it to you straight."

I wasn't sure what she meant, but I nodded again. "Okay."

She found a log beside the trail and sat down. I sat next to her and waited.

"Remember yesterday when I told you guys about Bob being a fisherman. Well, things were pretty good then—most of the time. We lived at the coast and I liked it there. I liked my school and I had a lot of friends. Bob hardly ever hit me, except when he drank too much. I usually stayed out of the way. One of my teachers saw some bruises on my arm and turned Bob and Serena in to Child Protective Services." Max sighed.

"It was the wrong thing to do," she continued. "Bob and Serena told the person they sent that I had fallen and she believed them. When she left, Bob told me if I ever did anything like that he'd let them take me. He said the only thing they could do to protect me was to move. We packed up and moved that night."

"Did you tell the lady that you hadn't fallen?"

"Are you kidding? There are some people you don't mess with. My uncle is one of them. Besides, I didn't want to go with her. Bob said they put kids like me in orphanages and treat us like prisoners. I'd been in that awful foster home, and no way was I going back. With Bob and Serena I can pretty much do what I want and go where I want." She shrugged. "Anyway, like I said, I know how to handle them most of the time. I should have known better than to accept the money from Serena—it was too much and . . . my fault. I'll know better next time."

I couldn't believe what I was hearing. "How can you say it's your fault? Adults should never hurt kids."

"Save it. I've heard all that garbage before. No way am I going to a foster home. Serena and Bob are my family. They take care of me and it isn't always like . . . like what you saw. They're pretty straight during the week. Besides, it won't be forever. I'll move out when I'm old enough to get my own place."

"When you're eighteen? Max, that's six years from now."

"Don't worry, Jess. I have places I can go and people who will help me out. There's a lady at the Goodwill who gives me really good deals on clothes and shoes." She hesitated. "It won't be like this for very long. I have a plan."

"What do you mean?" I didn't like the tone of her voice.

"Just what I said."

"Max." I looked up at her. "I still think you should turn Bob and Serena in."

"No, and you won't either. Not if you want to be my friend." She took hold of my shoulders again. "Promise me, Jessie Miller. Promise you won't tell anyone—not the teachers or your parents. Nobody. You got that?"

"Okay," I heard myself say. "For now. But if you get hurt again . . ."

"I won't." She let go and folded her arms. Her cheek was still red and swollen. The area around her eye was turning a bluish green.

"I—um—you can stay at my house anytime you want." I

wanted to protect Max, and if I couldn't tell anyone about her situation, I could at least give her a way out.

"Thanks." She smiled at me. "I appreciate that."

Life settled down for Max for a while—or maybe she was just putting on an act. She went back to being her funny, colorful self. As for me, things were anything but settled. More than anything, I wanted to tell my parents what I had learned about Serena and Bob Schultz. The promise I'd made to Max rolled around my stomach like bad, undigested food. I'd made the wrong choice in promising not to tell, and my conscience wasn't about to let me forget it.

What could I do? I had told Max I'd keep her secret for now, but I'd also made a promise to myself—if Max showed up with bruises again, I was telling my parents.

I didn't have to wait long. The next Saturday Max met me at the park, wearing a large baggy sweatshirt. That in itself was not unusual. What clued me in was the fact that the sun was shining and by noon the temperature had risen to 75 degrees. I could see the sweat breaking out along her hairline, but she wouldn't take off the heavy sweatshirt.

"It happened again, didn't it?" I asked.

Max clamped her mouth shut and set her jaw.

"You can't stay there, Max. Can't you see that? You may not want to be in foster care, but isn't that better than what you have now? I'm telling my parents."

"If you do, I'll never speak to you again. We'll have to move, and I don't want that. I like it here." She bit into her lower lip. "Please, Jess. Just give me a little more time. I almost got them talked into going into a rehab program. If they get off drugs, they'll be okay."

I turned away from her. "I can't promise. It's tearing me apart and—it's just wrong."

Max looked at me like I was the reason for all her troubles and tore off on her bike.

CHAPTER SEVEN

At school, Max made it clear that she no longer considered me a friend. It hurt to have her ignore me and to act like I didn't exist. Others noticed too. Ivy stopped me in the hall one morning before class. "What's with Max?" Ivy wrinkled her nose. "I mean, she's always a twit, but she's even acting mean toward you. I thought you two were friends."

I shrugged. "You'd have to ask her."

"I was just wondering . . . Do you want to walk home with me after school?" Ivy tugged her short knit top down to cover the top of her hip huggers. I wondered why she wore them. She wasn't fat, but the pants made her look that way. I wondered if she knew that. Then I thought, of course she does, but it doesn't matter. She wants to dress like her friends. I might have worn that style too, but I didn't have any hips to hold them up. Consequently, I wore jeans—boy's slims, which were the only kind that fit.

"Uh . . ." I didn't know what to say. I didn't want her to think that Max and I weren't friends anymore. Still, it would be nice to have someone to walk home with. "Sure," I finally said. "Why not?"

"Good. I'll meet you out front right after school." She smiled. "I like your hat."

"Thanks." I reached up to feel it. Mom had gotten the multi-colored yarn on her trip to the city to buy painting supplies. She'd knitted the colorful hat in one evening and promised me it wouldn't be itchy. So far she was right. It was made with that wild new fuzzy yarn. I probably wouldn't wear it for long—I never did. I couldn't get used to having my head covered with anything but my own hair. Mostly I put it on in the morning to keep my head warm.

When Ivy left, I finished pulling my books out of the locker and headed for math. School was easy—almost too easy. Mom said it was because she'd put me on an advanced track at home. I asked her about getting moved up a grade, but she thought I'd fit in better with kids my own age, especially with my being so small.

I doubted I'd ever fit in with anybody. I thought about Ivy and wondered if she was being sincere. Maybe she wanted to talk to me about Max. Maybe she and her friends were playing some kind of dirty trick. On one hand I was glad Ivy had asked me. On the other I felt guilty, like I was siding with the enemy. I wondered what Max would think. After school I did meet Ivy, and we walked home together. Max rode her bike past us, pretending like she didn't see us. I said hi, but she didn't answer.

"She's really been acting weird lately," Ivy said. "Even more than usual."

"Yeah. Maybe something is wrong at home." *Maybe she's just tired of being treated like an outsider. Maybe she's tired of hanging around me.*

"How did you do on the math quiz today?" Ivy asked, changing the subject.

I watched Max put the kickstand down on her bike and go into one of the shops on Main Street. "I did okay."

"I thought it was awful. It isn't fair of Mrs. Peters to give us tests on stuff we don't know."

I nodded and tried to sound like I cared. "I guess. Maybe she won't count it. Maybe she just wanted to see what we needed help in before school lets out."

"You're so good at math." Ivy sighed. "You're good at all your subjects."

"Thanks." I smiled, embarrassed to be talking about my grades. "I do okay."

"You don't like me very much, do you?" Ivy asked.

I glanced over at her, not sure how to answer. "I used to until you started treating me like a space alien." My tone was sharper than it needed to be. I had the feeling Ivy was trying to be friends again, but I wasn't sure I wanted to be friends with her.

"I'm sorry." Ivy sighed. "You were so different after your treatments and I didn't know how to act around you."

"It's all right. Forget I said anything." For the rest of the way home we talked about school and how it would be over soon. And what our plans were for summer vacation.

"I'm going to England on a buying trip with my mother," Ivy said.

"That sounds nice. We're supposed to go to Disney World." I didn't tell her that the trip was going to be sponsored by the Make-A-Wish Foundation. They were making it possible for my family to take me. I just hoped I lasted that long.

CHAPTER EIGHT

On a Sunday, I got sick again. With a disease like mine there are good times and bad. I go into remission and can feel good for a long time. Then I get too many bad white cells and my immune system starts shutting down. My doctor keeps a close watch on me. When I get sick, I end up in the hospital in isolation so I won't get a cold or the flu. Doctor Caldwell gave me the usual lecture about letting her know sooner. She was right. I should have told Mom to call her a couple of weeks ago.

For the last few weeks, I had felt myself getting weaker and weaker. Stress doesn't help and I'd had a lot of that lately. I had carried Max's secret with me all that time. Every day I would decide I had to tell Mom and Dad, and every day I'd back down. I don't know why. Maybe I just didn't want Max to be mad at me, but that was dumb because Max still wasn't talking to me. Maybe she thought that if she was mean to me, I'd forget about her and not care about her anymore. That wasn't going to happen.

I'm not sure how Max found out about my being in the

hospital, but the next day she came in with a lopsided wildflower bouquet, acting like we were still best friends.

"What are you doing here?" I asked. "I thought you didn't like me anymore."

"You can't just stop being friends." Max set the vase on the bedside stand. "Anyway, since no one from Child Protective Services has shown up, I figured you haven't told anyone. I wanted to thank you."

"I haven't, but that doesn't mean I won't."

"Well, you don't have to. Bob and Serena are getting help. They'll be going to rehab once a week."

I knew Max well enough to know she was lying. She had this habit of not looking at me. I didn't say anything. It felt good having her there, and I didn't want us to argue. I had also come to the conclusion that as fearless as Max seemed, she was not strong enough to handle her home situation alone. Unfortunately, at the moment, I was in no position to help her.

That night I told my parents what I should have told them weeks ago. Max was being abused.

Dad frowned. "Jessie, that's a pretty serious allegation. Are you sure?"

I nodded. I explained about the bruises I had seen on Max and how Serena had punched her in the face.

My mom hugged me. "How long have you known about this?"

"For a while. She keeps telling me things are better. I don't know if I believe her." I watched the fluid drip from the bag on an IV pole into the tubing.

"You did the right thing by telling us, Jessie." Dad's brown eyes connected with mine. "Secrets like that can only get worse."

I wasn't so sure. I felt terrible about keeping her secret, but I felt even worse now.

"I'll call social services first thing in the morning," Mom told me. "They'll send someone out to evaluate the situation."

"Max will hate me."

"Maybe for a while. But she'll get over it." Mom leaned over and kissed my forehead, pushing my imaginary hair back.

Would she? Max might never speak to me again, but at least she'd be safe. No kid should have to live in an abusive situation. I told them what Max had said about the foster home experience she'd had and how she was afraid of them.

Mom glanced at my dad, then back at me. "That poor child. No wonder she's so confused. I know there are some problems, but most foster home situations are good."

Mom did call Child Services, and they told her they would send someone out to investigate.

I didn't see Max for the next two days, and the waiting made my stomach ache. What if they had moved away? I'd lose Max forever.

On Wednesday Doctor Caldwell told me I could go home. I felt good. Amazing what blood and platelet transfusions can do for you.

I went back to school on Thursday but didn't see Max all day. I asked several of the teachers, but they hadn't seen her either.

After lunch, Cooper came up to me. "Do you know where Max is?"

The question surprised me. "Not for a couple of days. Have you seen her?"

"No." He seemed upset.

"Is something going on between you and Max?" I asked.

"It's none of your business," he shot back.

I shrugged and headed for class. When the last bell rang I practically ran over to Max's house. I rang the doorbell, afraid they were no longer there, afraid I had made a terrible mistake. *Please let her still be here.*

No one answered the door, so I walked into town and stopped at the beauty shop where Serena worked.

A bell dinged as I opened the door.

"Can I help you?" A woman with skin the color of chocolate milk and streaked blonde hair was bent over a sink, washing a customer's hair. There was no one else in the room.

I let the door close behind me. "Um—I'm looking for Serena."

"So am I, sugar." The woman, probably Jillian, went back to scrubbing her client's head. "Serena didn't come in today or yesterday. She hasn't called and she's not answering her phone. If you see her you can tell her for me, she doesn't need to bother coming back."

I thanked her and left. Jillian's beauty shop was only three doors down from the Cavanaughs' tea shop where Max and I had been nearly a month ago. I went in and sat down at the same table we'd shared then. *What have I done? I should never have told Mom and Dad. I'm sorry, Max. I'm so sorry.*

"Did you want something?" Ivy Cavanaugh put a menu in front of me. I looked at it, then at her. "I'd like some tea."

"What kind?" Ivy's eyes were filled with concern.

"Lavender infused Lady Grey," I said, remembering that Max had ordered it. Calculating the amount of money I had in my pocket, I ordered a scone to go with it.

She stood there for a while looking like she wanted to say something. "I heard you were in the hospital," she finally said. "Are you okay now?"

"For now. See, having leukemia is a little like having the life sucked out of you by a vampire. Every once in a while you gotta go in for new blood."

I could tell by the look on her face that I'd totally grossed her out. Good. I wasn't in the mood for pity. I wasn't in the mood to talk to anyone either. When she left, I heaved a deep sigh and stared out the window. I swallowed back the lump in my throat. Had they really moved away? What would I do without Max?

I left the tea shop half an hour later and walked home. Sam was outside playing with Brian Davidson and his twin brother Benjamin from next door. I felt jealous for a minute. The boys were having a water fight. It wasn't the water that got to me. It was the laughing and the fun time they were having. Max and I used to laugh about stuff.

I gathered up my pillow and quilt and settled onto the swing on the deck, watching them and wondering if I would ever see my friend again.

"Jessie. It's almost dinnertime." The swing moved as Mom sat on it.

I yawned and rubbed my eyes. "Is Max here?" I wasn't sure why I had asked. Wishful thinking, maybe.

"No. Were you expecting her?" Mom reached over to stroke my head. When I was little she used to brush the hair out of my eyes. There was no hair now, but I think she still does it out of habit.

"Not really. I was hoping." I used the back of the seat to pull myself up. "I think Max is gone."

"Gone?" Mom moved off the swing so I could push the covers away and swing my legs over the edge. "I think they might have moved. I shouldn't have told you about Bob and Serena."

Mom sat down beside me and spread out her arms. I leaned into them.

"The woman from Child Services called me back today." Mom wrapped her arms around me and patted my back. "She went to the house and talked to Max's aunt and uncle. Everything seemed okay, and Max told her it was all a big misunderstanding."

My lower lip started quivering, so I sucked it into my mouth. When I felt like I could talk, I said, "They moved. I went by the beauty shop and Serena wasn't there. Jillian said she hadn't been there or called."

"I'm sorry, honey. I had no idea. Maybe I can call the police."

"No." I jerked away. "You've done enough." I ran into the house, leaving Mom sitting there alone. I knew she felt bad, but I didn't care. I felt worse.

Friday after school I made one more effort to find Max. I rode my bike into Lakeside and went into the grocery store. "Is Bob Schultz here?" I asked the first checker I came to.

"He's working in produce," the woman said.

"So he's here?" I asked.

She smiled and nodded. "You can go back there if you want."

"Thanks." I wanted to jump up and down and dance. They hadn't moved away after all. I ran back to the produce section. Though I had never seen Bob, it wasn't hard to pick him out. His name was stitched on the apron he wore. He was arranging boxes of strawberries. I swallowed back my fear and approached him. "Those look like good berries."

He smiled at me. "Sure are. Locally grown. We just got them in today."

I smiled back. "I'll have to tell my mom." I wanted more than anything to ask him about Max. I hauled in a deep breath. "You're Alice Hunter's uncle, aren't you?"

His smile faded. "Who wants to know?"

"Um—I'm a friend of hers from school. She hasn't been there for a couple days, and I was worried."

"Humph." He frowned. "She's sick. Has the flu or something."

"So she's at home?"

"Last I heard."

"Do you think I could stop by and see her?"

"I wouldn't—not if you don't want to catch anything." He looked me up and down. "You don't look like you need a flu bug."

"I guess not."

Feeling relieved, but not quite thrilled, I left the store and pedaled back home. Once inside, I called Max's place. Max answered.

"It's you." I almost started crying. "What happened to you? I was afraid you'd moved away. I'm so sorry."

"Hey, it's okay. I talked them out of going."

"I went by your place, but nobody answered the door and Serena wasn't at work and . . ."

"Get a grip, Jess. I'm fine. Serena's been sick."

"I stopped by where she works and Jillian told me she hadn't called. I think she's lost her job."

"She didn't. She went back to work this afternoon."

"Can you come over?" I had to see her.

Max hesitated.

"Did they hurt you again?"

"It doesn't matter. What matters is that I have a plan. I could use your help—that is, if you're up to it."

"Sure." I sighed. "Anything."

"Invite me to spend the night at your place tonight."

"Okay." I was beginning to get that tight feeling in my stomach again. A warning telling me I was slipping into dangerous territory and I'd better back away. But I had come too close to losing my best friend, and I wasn't going to let that happen again. I put my hand over the mouthpiece and told my mother that I wanted Max to spend the night.

"Jessie . . ." She paused to look at me, and her resolve faded. Mom had a hard time saying no to me. "I thought you said Max was gone."

"She's still here. Please, Mom. It's important." I usually didn't take advantage of her weakness, but this was different.

"All right. As long as you get to bed early and do your homework."

"We will." I just hoped Max didn't have some late-night expedition planned.

Max showed up wearing new jeans and a tank top with an unzipped Husky sweatshirt. I stared at her. "Max, your hair?" Her wild, spiky, colorful hair had been shaved off.

"What?" She stepped around me and into the living room. "You think you're the only one around here who gets to go with the hairless style?"

"It's not a style." I stepped inside and closed the door.

"Sure it is. I saw a bald singer on television the other night and told Serena to give me a buzz cut."

"You went bald so I wouldn't feel alone, didn't you?" As soon as the words left my mouth I knew I was wrong.

"Sheesh." Max's gaze drifted to the floor. "You think the world revolves around you or something? My hair was like straw from all the dye jobs I've had."

I didn't believe her. Another possibility slipped into my head. "Serena shaved your head, but you didn't ask her to."

Max looked away. "You have a wild imagination. I happen to like my head shaved."

As always, Max was making the most of the situation. I could only imagine what it must have felt like for her. She loved those crazy and colorful hairstyles of hers. They were part of what made her so outrageous. How humiliating for her. How cruel of Serena.

"You can tell me the truth, Max."

"Yeah, and have you tell your parents—no way."

"I won't say anything." I wouldn't have to. Mom would know the minute she saw Max.

Mom and Sam had gone to the grocery store to pick up some things for dinner, and Dad hadn't come home yet. Max and I went out through the patio door and headed down to the dock.

"Can we take the boat out?" Max asked.

"Sure. Just make sure you don't row out too far. I'm not the best rower."

"I'll do it."

"We have to use the life jackets."

She pulled an orange jacket out of the box and tossed me a

yellow one. I climbed into the lightweight aluminum boat and sat on one of the three benches.

We rowed out about a hundred feet from shore before Max put the oars in the locks. She leaned back against the box that held the other life jackets. Hands behind her head, she closed her eyes. "Feels good being out here."

"It does." I dipped my hands in the water and made little swirls.

We sat there for a long time just breathing the cool mountain air and taking in the beautiful scenery. Chenoa Lake covered about ten thousand acres. The three small towns were situated at the north end. The rest of the perimeter was protected forestland. There were several islands on the lake, and at the south end the water drained out into Chenoa River. In all the years we'd lived there, we'd never explored the entire lake.

After a while Max sat up. "You were right, Jess. Serena shaved off all my hair while Bob held me down. I was too ashamed to go to school. Serena wasn't sick. Bob knocked her around after he was done with me. All because your mother called Child Protective Services."

"It's not fair to blame my mom. If you had told the social worker the truth, they would have taken you out of there."

"You still don't get it, do you? I don't want to go to a foster home. But none of that matters. The real problem is the drugs. I'm going to find out who their suppliers are. I'll tell Detective Johnson, and he'll close them down. Bob and Serena won't be able to buy the stuff anymore."

I wanted to tell her it would never work but couldn't make myself say it. Stopping the supply wouldn't end the problem, but Max had convinced herself that she'd found an answer.

"You want to back out?" she asked.

"No. I'm with you." And I would be, every step of the way. Max didn't always make the best decisions, and there was no way I'd let her handle a job like this alone. Over the next few minutes she outlined her plan in detail. While I doubted anything would end Bob and Serena's drug use, Max's plan would hopefully eliminate one more drug dealer. What I didn't tell her was that if I had anything to do with it, Bob and Serena would be arrested as well.

CHAPTER TEN

When Sam called us in for dinner, Max rowed back to shore. The steak, potatoes, and salad we had may as well have been cardboard for the way they felt in my mouth. I ate a few bites and slid the rest of my food around, making it look like I'd eaten something. My conscience twisted itself into a hundred knots, all designed to stop me from making another huge and dangerous mistake. I wouldn't listen.

Max ate everything on her plate and took seconds.

Sam thought it was cool that Max had the same haircut as mine. Max joked about it like she had with me.

The evening went by fast with each of us having to catch up on the work we'd missed at school. We were in bed by nine. Mom kissed us both good night. "Max, it's good to have you here. You're always welcome. You know that, don't you?"

I smiled. Mom was so transparent.

"Thanks, Mrs. Miller."

I lay in bed a long time, trying to go to sleep. My body was tired, but my brain wouldn't shut down. I kept thinking about

Max and her crazy ideas. And my own idiotic decision to go along with her.

I have one of those trundle beds with a mattress that you pull out, and Max was lying on it next to me. "You asleep?" she asked.

"No."

She sighed. "You go to church, don't you?"

"Yes." I wondered where she was headed with her questions.

"Do you believe in God?"

"Of course. Do you?"

"I used to before my mom and dad died. I don't know anymore. Bob and Serena don't."

"Maybe you could come to church with me," I said. "Check it out for yourself."

"Maybe I will." She was quiet for a while, then lifted up her head. "Could you pray for Serena and Bob? Maybe God will listen to you. He sure doesn't listen to me."

"Sure. But all the prayers in the world aren't going to make your aunt and uncle give up drugs unless they decide they want to stop."

"God won't stop them?"

"No." I rested my chin on my bony wrists. "It's complicated. Has something to do with free will."

"Are you saying it doesn't do any good to pray?"

"Of course not. God answers all our prayers, just not always the way we think He should."

Pretty soon I heard her slow, steady breathing. I said an extra prayer for Max and her family and eventually fell asleep.

Max went home right after breakfast on Saturday morning, saying she'd call me later and we'd put her plan into action. It's a wonder I didn't develop an ulcer while I waited.

CHAPTER ELEVEN

"It's time," Max said when I picked up the phone Saturday after-noon. I'd just finished an English paper and taken a nap.

"Time for what?" I pretended not to know what she was talk-ing about.

"They're gone. Meet me in front of the tea shop in five min-utes. And bring your cell phone."

I told my mother I was going into town and wanted to take the cell with me in case I needed her to pick me up.

"Are you feeling okay?" She felt my forehead.

"I'm okay, just a little tired."

Mom got that worried look. "I'd better make an appointment for you to see Dr. Caldwell. We should get your blood checked again."

"Okay. Just not today." I put the phone in one of the zippered pockets of my pants as I headed for the door. Once outside, I jumped on my bike and pedaled so fast I was out of breath when I put my bike into the stand. My legs ached and felt a little like Jell-O. For a minute I wasn't sure I could stand up.

Max was already there, sitting on a bench. I sat down beside her to catch my breath.

"You okay?" she asked.

"Yeah." I panted. "Just a little out of breath."

"You can stay out here if you need to."

"No," I said. "I'll come with."

She turned to face me. "There they are. Don't look. They're parking. I don't want them to see us." She looked back toward the shop. "They're going inside," she whispered.

This was the first really good look I'd gotten at Serena since that awful day I saw her in her bathrobe yelling at Max. Today she looked like a model, with her curly blonde hair and a slim-fitting sundress and matching sandals.

"Are you ready?" Max nudged me.

I'd never be ready, but I nodded anyway.

The shop was one I'd gone into lots of times. When family and friends visited they always wanted souvenirs. I knew the people who owned the shop and didn't figure them for drug dealers, but these days, you never knew. Of course, anything was possible since they hardly ever worked in the store themselves. They had a manager and several employees.

We sneaked in—actually, we just walked in, cause you couldn't sneak. A bell dings when someone comes in or out. Anyway, we walked in and stepped to the right, behind a rack of sweatshirts.

The clerk glanced in our direction, but then went on talking to Bob. Serena was looking at a cute T-shirt with a picture of an angel on it. "Your order is in the storeroom," the clerk said. "Come on back and check it out."

"See, I told you," Max whispered, ducking down so her aunt and uncle couldn't see her.

"The 'order' could be anything. What makes you think it's drugs?"

"I just know," Max said. "Let's go back so I can get a look at them."

I shook my head. "No way. They'll see us for sure."

"You're right. That would mess things up. I need to get closer though, so I can at least hear them. Did you bring your cell phone? We'll need to call the cops so they can catch them red-handed."

I nodded as my hand closed around the phone. My way of escape if we got into trouble.

We made our way to the back of the shop, stopping next to a rack of screen-printed T-shirts like the one Serena had been looking at earlier. The winged creature I thought was an angel turned out to be a fairy, lighting on a flower.

The clerk came out of the back room with a foot-square box and set it on the counter. "This is the last one."

"Are there more coming in?" Bob asked.

He shook his head. "Not this time." He rang up the purchase and Bob handed him a credit card. I thought it was strange—Bob buying drugs with a credit card—but I didn't say anything.

We waited in the store, pretending to be shoppers, until Bob and Serena left. The clerk kept looking at us like we were shoplifters or something. I could tell he wanted us out of there. After a few minutes, Max grabbed a candy bar from the shelf near the register and paid for it.

The clerk was a guy in his twenties. His name badge read "Danny Edwards." "Have a nice day," he said in a sarcastic tone. The bell jingled as we left the store. Max didn't stop until we got to the end of the block.

"Give me the cell," she demanded.

I dug it out of my pocket. "What are you going to do?"

"Call the cops. That guy just sold my aunt and uncle a box of drugs."

"I don't know, Max. Doesn't it seem kind of weird that the guy would ring up the sale and then accept a charge card?"

"No." Max punched in 911. "Don't you get it? They bought a statue. The statue is full of cocaine or something."

"What? You have X-ray eyes? You can see through boxes?" I was really getting irritated.

"Trust me, Jess. They've done this before." Apparently someone answered the phone, cause she held up a hand for me to be quiet.

I sighed and went to sit on a bench a few feet away, listening to Max describe the shop and tell them that the clerk had drugs in the back room. My stomach hurt again, and I had a feeling things were not going to go as she'd planned. If she was right, what would happen to the package Bob and Serena already had?

A few minutes later the same detective who'd found us in the warehouse pulled up in front of the gift shop. Detective Johnson was in the store maybe five minutes before he came out. He saw us sitting on the bench and headed our way.

"We're in trouble," I said.

"No, we're not. He just wants to thank us for the tip."

The scowl on his face told me I was right, but I had no intention of arguing with Max. Besides, I didn't have time to say anything.

"You called in that anonymous tip, didn't you, Max?"

Max leaned back and looked up at him. "What if I did? Did you find the stash?"

"We didn't find anything. And we don't have enough evidence for a search warrant." He hunkered down in front of us.

"So you didn't go into the back room?"

"What makes you think there are drugs in there?"

"I overheard the clerk tell these people their shipment came in. He took them to the back room and they came out with this box. They didn't open it or anything but . . ."

Detective Johnson shook his head.

"It had to be drugs," Max told him. "What else would it be?"

He rubbed the back of his neck like I've seen my father do when he's exasperated. "These people get shipments all the time. They own a gift shop, for Pete's sake. I know you want to be good citizens, but harassing shop owners isn't the way to do it."

"But . . ."

"Leave it alone, okay? I don't want to see you kids getting

hurt." He shook his head. "Police work is serious business. It can be dangerous. I thought you learned your lesson at the warehouse the other day. If we hadn't been there, those guys might have killed you."

Max had a set to her jaw that said she had no intention of giving up. As for me, I sat there swinging my skinny legs, scared to death we'd end up in jail. "We didn't mean to cause any trouble," I said. "We were just trying to help."

"That kind of help we don't need. This wild goose chase just cost the taxpayers a few thousand dollars in manpower, wages, and paperwork."

I opened my mouth to comment, but Max beat me to it. "No way."

"Yes way. It costs a lot of money to check out a tip. Keep that in mind next time you think you've found a drug dealer. Now, I want you two to do whatever kids your age do. No more looking into criminal activity, no more drug investigations. You leave that to us."

More than anything I wanted to tell him about Serena and Bob, but I knew Max would kill me. She wanted the drugs stopped, but didn't want to turn in her aunt and uncle.

"Okay," I said.

He turned to Max, who shrugged her shoulders. "What if we see a place being robbed or somebody being mugged? Is it okay to call you then?"

He smiled. "Come on, Max, you know the difference."

She smiled back. "Just so we're clear."

He left then and the butterflies in my stomach began to settle down. At least they did until I looked over and noticed Danny Edwards, the clerk from the gift shop, scowling at us. "He knows it was us, Max." My breath caught in my throat. "He knows it was us who called the police."

CHAPTER TWELVE

Max glanced at the clerk just as he ducked inside. "Great." She began chewing on her lower lip. "I can't go home. I know he'll call Bob and Serena. He'll tell them it was me."

"Does he even know who you are?"

She nodded. "I think so. If he doesn't, they'll be able to figure it out. How many girls do you know with bald heads?"

She had a point. I was afraid to go home too. The clerk didn't know me, but the store owner sure did. A call to my parents would probably result in my being grounded or worse. I'd never gotten into trouble before I met Max. Maybe that's because I was too busy being sick and getting well again to worry about making the wrong choices. Of course, part of it was seeing how difficult things were for Mom and Dad when Sam acted up or when I got sick. I didn't want to upset them more than they already were.

"Come stay overnight with me," Max said. "If you're with me, they won't do anything."

I got up and headed for my bike. "I don't know if that's a good idea. Why don't you just stay at my place?"

"I can't. They'll expect me to be home tonight."

"How can you be sure they won't hurt me too?"

"They won't." Max didn't seem too sure. "They're always nice around other people."

"I need to go home first. I'll make sure it's okay with Mom and Dad."

"I'll come with you."

As it turned out, my parents wouldn't let me stay at Max's place. They didn't feel comfortable, and to be honest, neither did I. But Mom called Serena at the beauty shop and asked her if Max could stay at our house.

"Serena said it was okay," Mom said when she hung up.

"Thanks, Mom." I gave her a hug, knowing she wanted both of us to be safe.

"I'll get my stuff and be right back." Max flashed Mom and me a big smile. "Thanks, Mrs. M."

"You're welcome."

After Max left, I thought about staying in the kitchen with Mom, but decided not to. She'd want to talk about Max, and I wasn't ready. We hadn't really talked about Mom's call to Child Services—the one that got Max a shaved head.

Mom would get this sad look in her eyes whenever she looked at Max. Like she wanted to take Max home for good. I wished I could do something, but like Max said, "Jessie, you've caused too many problems already. Please don't try to help me anymore."

Then she had laughed and added, "With friends like you, who needs enemies?"

I didn't think it was funny. Still don't. She says I don't understand, and I guess that's true.

While I waited for Max to come back, I curled up on the porch swing and fell asleep listening to the sound of water lapping on the shore and birds chirping in the trees.

I woke up when I heard the phone ringing and my mother answering. "Oh, hi, Dr. Caldwell. What's up?" Her voice carried through the screen on the door, and pretty soon she was standing beside me.

I yawned, but didn't get up. I felt tired and wished I could have slept longer.

"That's good news. I'll be sure to tell her." Mom nodded as though the caller could see her. I smiled at that.

"What did Dr. Caldwell want?" I asked when she pressed the button to end the conversation.

Mom squeezed in beside me and ran her hand over my head like she was brushing the hair out of my eyes again. "You'll be up for a bone marrow transplant soon. She thinks she may have found a donor."

"Really?" In a way it was good news, but it would mean going back to the hospital again. That didn't excite me. Mom and Dad felt bad that their blood and mine weren't compatible. Both of them would have volunteered in a flash. The only one in the family who could have been a donor was Sam, and he was way too young. You should have seen him when he found out. He cried and cried. Guess he thought that if I couldn't get the marrow from him I'd die. Anyway, I got put on the list. Now I'd get marrow from a stranger. "Did she say when?"

"No. Hopefully within a month. When school's out."

I groaned. "That's not the way I thought I'd be spending my summer vacation."

"I know, honey. I'm sorry."

"What about Max? Who's gonna . . ." I caught myself, but it was too late.

"Who's going to what? Keep her out of trouble? Keep her safe?" Mom sighed. "Honey, you're not responsible for Max."

"I know, it's just . . ." I almost told her about Max's obsession to stop the drug dealing. I guess that's why I was so afraid for her. What if she confronted the wrong people? What if she went too far?

Mom gently squeezed my hand. "Maybe things will change for her between now and then."

I doubted they would. Max would never give up. Then I wondered if she might. If I was really honest with myself I'd admit that what scared me more than anything was that Max might follow in Bob and Serena's footsteps and start doing drugs herself. What if they forced her to take drugs with them? I made myself stop thinking about it and focused hard on my mother's words.

"The important thing is to take care of yourself," Mom went on. "We want you around for a long time to come." She leaned over and kissed my forehead, tears glistening in her blue eyes.

The front doorbell rang and Mom went to answer it.

I twisted around to sit up. Max must be back.

"She's out on the deck," I heard Mom say.

The person who pushed open the screen door wasn't Max at all.

"Hi, Jessie." Ivy glanced at me briefly and then looked out at the water.

"Hi," I said. "What are you doing here?" I wished I could have pulled back the question, but it was too late. I laughed. "That didn't come out right."

"It's okay. I know I haven't been over here in a while."

I shoved my blanket aside. "Want to sit down?"

"Sure." Ivy settled onto the swing and set it into motion. "I . . . uh . . . I was wondering if you wanted to come to my birthday party. It's Saturday, May 27th, at my house."

That was two weeks away. "Really?" I wasn't sure what to say. I wanted to go, and it had been a long time since I'd been invited anywhere. "Are you sure?"

She looked at me funny. "I wouldn't have asked if I didn't mean it. Actually, I'm inviting all the girls in our class. It'll be like a graduation party—getting out of sixth grade." She pulled her fingers through her silky hair.

My hair used to be like that, soft and silky. I looked away, trying to talk past the sudden lump in my throat. "Sounds like fun, but I'll have to ask my parents. What time?"

"We're having a sleep-over, so we'll have a pizza picnic in the backyard and sleep outside." Her wide mouth spread into a smile, revealing a set of braces.

"Are those new?" I shouldn't have asked. I knew they were and that she was still not used to them.

"Uh-huh. They're to correct my overbite. They hurt all the time, but the dentist says I'll get used to them. I hope so."

Max banged out the door and stopped short when she saw Ivy sitting beside me. Her smile faded, and I thought I saw a glimpse of anger. Then the smile came back when she saw the horror in Ivy's eyes. I saw it too. She was looking at Max's bald head. I knew Ivy wanted to say something, but she didn't. I liked her for that.

"Hey, Ivy, what are you doing in the slums?"

I didn't like Max's comment, but didn't say so. I guess next to Ivy's mansion, our house must have looked plain.

"I was just inviting Jessie to my birthday party." Ivy looked at me, then back at Max. "You can come, too, if you want."

I wondered if Ivy would have asked Max if she hadn't come by just then. She'd said she planned to invite all of the girls in the sixth grade, but had she meant to include Max? I guessed she had, otherwise why invite me?

Max didn't answer right away, and I wished I could have read her mind. Max sort of prided herself on not being part of the group.

"I'll have to think about it." Max dropped down on the deck facing Ivy and me, her legs folded in a yoga position.

Ivy gripped her lower lip between her teeth. "I hope you can." She told Max about the sleep-over.

Max shrugged. "Sure. Why not?"

I felt relief and foreboding all at once. The look in Max's eyes spelled trouble with a capital T.

CHAPTER THIRTEEN

I tried to talk to Max about that look after Ivy left and while we were rowing on the lake.

"What are you talking about?" she asked innocently. "I'm not planning anything weird."

"You're going to put worms in their sleeping bags, aren't you? Or use the water hose to put out the candles on the cake. Or . . ."

Max laughed so hard she nearly rocked the boat over. "I love it. And here I thought *I* was the bad girl."

I giggled, happy to hear her laughter. "You forget, I have a little brother. Sam is adorable, but he's always playing tricks. Besides, maybe I've been around you too long."

She got serious then and scooped up the oar she'd dropped into the water. "Why do you think she asked us?"

I told Max that Ivy and I used to be friends before my first bout of chemo. "I think she was afraid of being around me."

"And now she wants to make up?"

"She's inviting all the girls in our class. But she's been nice to me lately."

"You know what I heard?"

I frowned, not sure where she was heading.

"I heard that Ivy and the other girls have decided to rescue you from me. They think I'm a bad influence."

"That's crazy. They don't care about me and . . ."

"I *am* a bad influence." Max tightened her grip on the oars and stroked hard, moving us closer to shore. "I get you into trouble and I tire you out. It's my fault you ended up in the hospital last time."

"No, it's not. I like hanging out with you."

"I don't want to be your friend anymore, kid. It just isn't working out."

I didn't know what to say. I sat there with my mouth open for the longest time. "Why are you doing this?"

Max shrugged. "I don't need you, Jess. I don't need anybody. I especially don't need friends who get me into trouble with Serena and Bob and whose parents call CPS."

Had Mom called CPS again? Had someone else? "They're moving, aren't they?"

Max rowed harder and I knew I'd hit a nerve.

"You don't have to go with them this time," I insisted.

"I told you before—there's no way I'm going to a foster home."

I stuck my hand in the water and stared at the trail my fingers left, how it spread out farther and farther. My father once told me that a tiny ripple can alter the ecosystem of the entire pond. I wondered how I would feel, the choices I would make, if my parents started using drugs. I didn't think I could ever turn them in, no matter how terrible things got. But then I wasn't as brave as Max, and I told her so.

"I'm not brave," she said.

"So you're just giving up?"

"They told me they were going to stop."

"And you believe them?" I knew Max wasn't that naive.

She ducked her head and stopped rowing. We drifted for a while. Max placed the oars across her lap. "No," she said after a while. "I don't believe them, but it's getting harder and harder for them to get the drugs. The police are cleaning up this whole area. There's a no-tolerance-on-drugs campaign. The sheriff says he's going to run the drug dealers out of town."

"Did you get into trouble with your aunt and uncle for turning in the guy at the store this afternoon?" I asked.

"I don't think they know." Max looked toward town. "Maybe he didn't tell them."

"What do you think they'll do when they find out?" I still couldn't look her in the eye. I felt betrayed and angry. How could she just decide that she didn't want to be my friend?

"Maybe they won't know it was me."

"The guy saw us, and like you said, how many other kids in town are bald?"

She shrugged.

"When are you moving?"

She shrugged again. "Maybe tonight. Maybe tomorrow. Maybe next week. It doesn't matter since I won't be hanging out with you anymore."

A plan began to formulate in my head. I couldn't tell Max about it. I couldn't tell anyone. Max wanted to stop her aunt and uncle from using drugs by cutting off their supplier. I knew that wasn't going to work. My plan, if it worked, would be much more drastic. Max might never speak to me again, but I had to do something. I was willing to sacrifice our friendship as long as I got Max away from them.

Max went home after dinner. She told my parents that she'd changed her mind about staying. I figured Serena had changed *her* mind. I didn't care really. In fact, not having Max there made my job easier.

I went to bed early and read until midnight. When I felt certain everyone was asleep, I grabbed a sweatshirt out of my closet and stuffed my feet into my tennis shoes. I quietly opened my closet door. I got out my nylon net beach bag to hold all the stuff I'd need: binoculars, a camera, a flashlight, some snacks for energy, my tape recorder, and a notepad. Before pulling the drawstring tight, I wrote a quick note to Mom and Dad in case something happened. *Gone to see Max. Love, Jessie.*

Careful not to make a lot of noise, I sneaked down the stairs, slid open the patio door, and stepped onto the deck. My heart stopped when the board under my foot creaked. After waiting several seconds to make sure no one had heard, I tiptoed down the stairs, then ran down to the lake where I eased the boat into the water and climbed in.

The wind had picked up a little. I shivered, glad I'd worn my hooded sweatshirt.

After putting the oars in the oarlocks, I slipped them into the water and maneuvered around until the front of the boat was facing toward town. Before beginning my journey, I tipped my head back and watched the stars twinkle against the night sky. The moon was full and bright—giving me plenty of light. "Please, God," I whispered, "help me do this. Make me strong enough to get there and back. And please let this work."

I had decided earlier that going by water would cut my travel time to Max's place in half. Plus, no one would see me. By the time I got to the beach access road, which was only about three blocks from Max's house, my arms felt like they were going to fall off. The current and the wind at my back had made the trip easier. I didn't want to think about the ride home, as I'd be going against the wind. Maybe it would shift by then.

My legs felt shaky as I pulled the aluminum boat up onto the sand and grabbed my bag. I'd only gotten halfway up the bank when my knees buckled and I fell. I lay there for a while, catching my breath and gathering up the courage to go on.

"Come on, Jessie," I said under my breath. "You can't give up now."

I rolled over and sat up. "This is a stupid idea," I muttered. "Even dumber than Max's plan to turn in the store owner for dealing drugs. What if they aren't home? What if nothing happens tonight?"

Then you go back tomorrow, I told myself. Besides, this was Saturday night, and the drug trade was big on weekends. At least that's what I'd heard. Some of the older kids went to raves where they used ecstasy and cocaine.

I rested for a few more minutes, then began the trek up the steep hill and on to the house where Max lived. The road leading from the beach was narrow and lined on both sides with concrete and stone walls to protect the property owners' privacy. Long strands of ivy had rooted themselves into the walls, creating a garden effect. At the top of the hill I crossed Cedar Street and kept going. At the end of the next block I turned right onto Ash. Serena and Bob's house was at the end of the block.

Every step brought with it a warning from somewhere in my head, telling me to go back. I pushed the warnings aside. I was not about to let Max leave with those people. Somehow, Bob and Serena had to be stopped. When I got to the driveway I ducked into some bushes. I guess I was half expecting to see a moving truck, but the only vehicle parked in the driveway was Bob's black van. The lights were on in the house and the drapes closed.

I walked up the drive and was just starting to go behind the house when a car pulled into the driveway. The headlights caught me. I ducked.

It had to be close to one in the morning, and here I was hunkered down behind a pair of garbage cans pleading with God to save me. I closed my eyes tight and held my breath when the driver cut the lights and opened the car door. He didn't seem in too much of a hurry, so I figured he hadn't seen me before I ducked out of sight. Maybe he thought I was an animal or something. I wasn't about to ask.

The man was tall and wiry, wearing jeans and a leather jacket. He had dark hair that curled around his collar and looked like he might be about Bob's age, which would have made him 30 to 35.

I'd seen him before, and when I realized where, I could hardly breathe. He was one of the guys who'd been arrested at the warehouse. He'd been in handcuffs then, but I know he'd have killed me if he'd had the chance. Now here I was, standing only twenty feet away at the most.

I fumbled around in my bag for my notepad and pen and jotted down a description of the guy and his car along with the license number. It was a red sports car, a newer model. I peered at the design on the grill and recognized the Mustang ornament. By now the guy had reached the front door. He knocked once, then reached for the doorknob and let himself in.

Reaching into my bag again, I snapped a picture of the car. The flash went off and sent a streak of panic straight through me. Had he seen it? Had someone else?

"Jessie," I said, hardly breathing. "You have to be more careful. One thing for sure—you make a terrible spy." I put the camera back, not sure what I should do next. My plan hadn't extended much beyond go to Max's place and look for any illegal activity, record it, and hand it over to the police. While Max was intent on keeping drugs away from her aunt and uncle, my plan was to find sufficient evidence to have them arrested. That way they wouldn't be able to move and Max would have to be taken away from them.

So far nothing illegal had taken place, except maybe for me snooping around Bob and Serena's house. I straightened and made my way to the back of the house, hoping I might be able to get a look inside. I'd never been inside the house, but I knew that from the front door I could see past the living room into the kitchen and that the kitchen door had a window. That's where I headed. From that window I should be able to get a good look at the living room and dining room, which was most likely where I'd find Bob and Serena and their guest.

Sure enough. I passed under a window that I imagined was a bedroom, probably Max's. Through the back door window I had a perfect view of the threesome. Fortunately, with the lights inside and the darkness outside, they couldn't see me.

The guy with the Mustang sat down at the dining room table with Bob. Serena came into the kitchen and I ducked. "Want something to drink, Cody?" she asked.

"Sure. Anything so long as it's cold." I raised up again as Serena pulled out three brown bottles, then pushed the refrigerator door shut with her foot. She set the bottles down in front of the two men and twisted the cap off her own. I scribbled the name Cody in my notebook.

Cody set a briefcase in the center of the table. "Made a big haul tonight," he said. "That party up at the old grange hall brought in a couple hundred kids. Sold all I had and could probably do more if you have it."

I gasped when I saw what was inside. The briefcase was full of money. I realized then that Serena and Bob weren't just users. They were also suppliers. I wanted to take a picture of them, but couldn't chance it. They'd see the flash for sure. The police would just have to accept my word for it. I scribbled information about the briefcase and the money into the notebook.

"We have a new shipment." Bob reached for a few bills and came up with a bunch of twenties. "But you're not going back there. By now the cops are all over the place."

"What do you mean?" Cody frowned, then leaned back and took a long drink.

"I mean that I talked to the sheriff at the store just before I came home, and he told me they planned to hit the grange tonight after midnight. I tried to call you on your cell, but couldn't get through."

Cody pulled a cell phone out of his pocket and peered at it. "Needs recharging."

"That's sloppy work, Cody. You could have still been there when the cops showed up."

Cody set the bottle down on the table. "Lucky for us, I wasn't. I left a few minutes before midnight."

Bob glanced at his watch. "And you're just now getting here?"

Cody put his hands behind his neck and arched back with a yawn. "Stopped to get some food. Selling this stuff works up an appetite."

"You're sure no one spotted you?" Serena reached into the briefcase for a handful of bills.

"Not a chance." He paused to light up a cigarette, then inhaled and blew out a gray billow of smoke.

The three of them sat there hunched over the table while they counted and stacked the bills.

I wasn't sure what I should do next. I'd heard enough to know these guys should be in jail, but I doubted my say-so would be enough for the police. Max and I had learned that much when we'd called Detective Johnson about the gift shop. The only thing a call to the cops would do now was to stir things up and send Bob, Serena, and Cody underground or possibly out of town— something I wanted to prevent.

I sat down on the back step. What did I really have on them?

Probably not enough to bring the police in. *They have a briefcase full of money they'd earned selling something. You don't even know what they were selling. They never said. Could be M&Ms for all you know.*

Discouraged, I decided to go back home. Maybe I'd talk to my parents about what I'd found. They'd be upset that I went out by myself, especially after all their lectures about not going out alone at night. I hadn't worried about that on the way here. Now their words haunted me. Suppose there was a stalker out there. Suppose someone had seen me and was waiting in the shadows.

I shook my head to clear it. I was safe enough here in Chenoa Lake. Wasn't I?

I headed back to the main road. The temperature had dropped, so I zipped up my sweatshirt and pulled the hood farther down on my head.

For a while, I wasn't sure I would have enough strength to make it back to the boat. My arms and legs felt like 50-pound weights. But I did get to the boat and into it. I pushed off and started rowing back to my house. The wind had picked up again, making all my hard paddling worthless. Cold and relentless, the wind swooped down from the mountain. Too late I realized the gusting wind had been pushing me away from shore. I rowed as hard as I could to get closer to land, but the lights kept getting farther and farther away.

Fifteen minutes later, I stopped rowing. My arms ached and I felt sick to my stomach. I lifted the oars and set them in the boat.

Just for a minute, I told myself. *Have to rest. Just for a minute.*

I curled up in the bottom of the boat, using my life jacket as a pillow, and closed my eyes.

CHAPTER FIFTEEN

When I woke up it was light and warm. The sun was shining, turning the back of my closed eyelids orange and red and yellow. I brought my arm up to shade my eyes and gasped at the pain the small movement made. *Why is the sun shining on me? Why is my bed so hard? Why do I ache all over?*

The thoughts tumbled around in my head before finally settling into an answer. All too soon, I remembered sneaking out of the house at midnight to spy on Bob and Serena. I'd stopped fighting against the wind and fallen asleep in the boat.

When I sat up the boat began rocking. I gripped the sides, praying I wouldn't be dumped overboard. Not that I was in any real danger of that. The water was smooth and clear now. As the boat settled, I looked around, expecting to see the familiar shoreline off to my left. There was nothing familiar about the land surrounding me. I was in some sort of cove with land on three sides and an inlet off to my right. I had no idea where I had drifted to. All I knew was that there were no houses and no sign of people anywhere.

I heard the flutter of wings behind me, and when I turned around I came face-to-face with a seagull. It started pecking at my bag, which I'd set near the prow.

"Shoo!" I waved a hand and he cocked his head from side to side as if expecting a handout. The trouble with seagulls is that once someone feeds them, they come to expect it. The scavengers could be a real nuisance.

I grabbed my bag and set it next to me. "Go!" I shouted this time, waving my arms at him.

He squawked in protest and fluttered his wings.

"You are not getting my granola bars."

He must have finally gotten the message because he flew away, coming to land on an outcropping of rocks. He eyed me with the same wary expression I gave *him*.

With the sun beating down on me, I was getting too warm. I pulled off my sweatshirt and stuffed it into my bag, then decided I'd better head for shore. I needed to find some shade so I wouldn't burn. I also needed to have a look around to see where I was. Hopefully, I'd be close enough to town so I could row back home.

Mom and Dad would be up now and wondering what had happened to me.

With every muscle in my body aching, I rowed to shore and pulled the boat up and out of the water. The cove was sheltered and heavily treed. Once the sleepiness had gone, I realized that I must have drifted out to one of the islands that spotted the lake.

Hooking the bag on my arm, I climbed up some rocks to a level spot where I could see beyond the cove. I saw land all right, but nothing remotely resembled the three small towns that crowded at the upper end of Chenoa Lake.

The land I did see was about half a mile away and I could have rowed to it. But I wouldn't. There was nothing there to greet me but trees, shrubs, deer, bear, cougar, and whatever other wildlife occupied the old-growth forest.

The wind had been blowing hard the night before. It, along with the current, must have swept me to the far side of the lake. *Just be glad the wind was blowing, or you might have gotten caught in the current and taken over the falls.* I shivered just thinking about it.

"I'm an idiot." I pulled up my knees and rested my arms on them, then used my fist to rest my chin. Mom and Dad would be way beyond worried. I thought about the note I'd written. No doubt they would have called Max by now. She'd be furious with me. They'd all be mad at me. And for what? I imagined myself telling them, "I saw this guy pull into Bob and Serena's place at 1:00 a.m. He and Serena and Bob hung out together, drinking, eating, and counting drug money . . ." I had nothing but my own suspicions. I knew they were dealing drugs, but had no way to prove it. And now I'd gotten myself lost.

I moved back to the tree line, away from sun, and sat down under a maple tree. "At least you brought some food," I told myself in a disgusted tone.

Sliding the bag from my shoulder, I pulled out one of the granola bars and peeled back the wrapper. I'd no sooner taken a bite when the seagull returned.

"Go away." I took a bite and chewed slowly, savoring the sweet, nutty taste.

The gull squawked at me and tipped his head from side to side, his beady eyes watching every move in case I dropped a crumb or something. I half expected him to take the bar right out of my hand. I started feeling guilty for eating in front of him and finally gave in. "Oh, all right." I broke off a small piece and tossed it at him.

He fluttered about for a minute capturing it and gulping the morsel down, then stared at me again.

"No more. This is going to have to last me until I get rescued. Which shouldn't take too long," I added, remembering the cell phone in my sweatshirt pocket.

I'm not sure exactly what happened then. I reached to my side to get my bag, when the seagull lunged at me. I screamed and put my arms up to shield my head. He screamed back and batted his wings against me, then fluttered wildly beside me. I managed to get up and back away. The gull tugged at my bag and I realized he'd gotten his beak caught in the net.

I watched him struggle, frantic to free himself. "If you'd hold still, I could help you." I softened my tone and reached toward him.

Wrong move. The bird lifted off and flew out over the water.

The weight of the bag must have pulled him down, because he plunged into the lake. Just when I thought he had drowned, he came up sputtering. He'd manage to free himself, but in the process he'd lost my bag.

I couldn't believe it. I'd been here ten minutes and the bird had stolen my food, my sweatshirt, and my cell phone. I sat back down under the tree, stunned. Panic rose in my chest, and I could almost feel it race through my veins.

Stay calm, Jessie, I told myself. *Think.*

CHAPTER SIXTEEN

I thought about Mom and Dad and how frantic they must be. By now, they had called Max, who had told them she hadn't seen me and had no idea where I was. Would she help them look for me? Mom and Dad would have called the police. They'd know the boat was missing and probably comb the shoreline. Why hadn't I just rowed to shore when I knew I couldn't make it all the way home? Then I remembered how the wind had blown me farther out into the lake and how tired I'd been.

You should have been able to make it home. Max would have . . . I stopped the thought right there. I was not Max. I was Jessie. Pathetic, bald, weak little Jessie. What had I been thinking? I should have known my limitations.

"Please, God, let them find me," I pleaded. "I'm sorry I went to Bob and Serena's. I'm sorry I took the boat out. Just please let them find me."

I felt better somehow. Praying did that to me sometimes. It was like handing my troubles over to God and letting Him worry about them. With renewed hope, I climbed off the rock and went back to the boat. There I grabbed the life jacket I'd been wearing and set it in plain view. Chenoa Lake was huge. Dad would most likely start the search near the shore, then spread out from there. If the sheriff sent up search-and-rescue planes or a helicopter, there was a good chance they'd spot the life jacket. I went back up to my perch under the tree, where I'd be able to see any boats in the area. Weekends brought out a lot of tourists and fishermen, but with a lake this big, what were the chances of anyone coming way out here?

Looking toward the sky, I made an amendment to my prayer. "Please let them find me before nightfall. One of Your stupid sea-gulls took my food and my sweatshirt." I sighed. "But then You already know that."

I sat for a long time, waiting, hoping, and praying. Finally, around noon, when the sun was directly overhead, I got up and walked around. My arms and legs were stiff and sore from the rowing and the walking I'd done the night before.

I had no idea how big the island was or if it was truly an island. I decided I should probably do some exploring. Maybe someone was camped nearby or even lived here. One or two of the islands were occupied during the summer. Of course it wasn't summer yet. Sitting on the rock all that time, I realized the only way anyone would see the boat was to fly directly over it. So far I hadn't heard or seen any planes. But then, probably no one expected me to be this far away from civilization. If I were looking for someone on the lake, I'd probably go to the islands closer in and do a thorough search there before fanning out.

Going through the woods seemed like a bad idea. I wanted to stay out in the open in case a search plane or boat came close enough to see me. That meant only one thing: I'd have to take the boat out of the cove and row around the island. Unfortunately, I didn't have the strength to do that.

For the first time in a long while I felt myself getting mad at God for giving me leukemia. Even as the thought entered my head, I could almost feel Mom's arms go around me. She'd start crying and hold me close and say something like, "Oh, Jessie, God doesn't want bad things to happen to us. But sometimes they do. Leukemia is one of the diseases people get." One time she told me that diseases are like the rain that comes into our lives. Rain doesn't discriminate, getting one person wet and leaving another dry. Of course, sometimes people suffer because of the choices they make. In my case, leukemia was just an ugly rain.

At the moment, all I wanted to do was lie down and take a nap. Only there was no place to sleep except on the ground. To be honest, I'd seen a few bugs and spiders and wasn't about to lie out on the bare ground. I shuddered just thinking about it. I could have laid out the other life jackets. I had four in all, but I didn't dare cover any part of them in case a plane flew over the area. I went back up to my tree and sat down. Then, leaning my head against the tree, I closed my eyes.

CHAPTER SEVENTEEN

I woke up sometime later. A long time later. The sun had slipped behind the mountains, and I could see the dull pinks and reds and yellows of a dying sunset. It would soon be dark and I was starting to get cold. And scared. Really, really scared. Being so skinny, I got chilled way too fast. I wondered how cold it would have to get and how long I would have to wait before hypothermia set in.

About the only thing I had to use as a covering were the life jackets. I hurried down to the boat and climbed inside and started rearranging the bright orange jackets. I placed two in the bottom of the boat to use as a mattress. Then, picking up a third, I put my head through the opening and secured the straps. I folded my arms in as far as I could. At least I hadn't worn just a tank top. I'd put a long-sleeved cotton knit shirt on over the tank. The last life jacket I placed against my right side, thinking I could move it to the other side if I got too cold.

My stomach growled, and I had a few not-so-nice thoughts about the seagull who'd stolen my snacks. At least I had water. A whole lake full of it. I wasn't sure how clean it was, but the tourist brochures claimed it was clean enough to drink. Only boats with small motors were allowed on the lake at all except for half-a-dozen licensed fishing boats and two cabin cruisers owned by the sheriff's department.

I filled my water bottle and drank half of it, then set it beside me. The back part of the vest served as a pillow as I lay down. I couldn't believe how tired I was. I knew my white count was up again, but I didn't want to think about that. I just wanted to sleep.

It wasn't quite dark when I closed my eyes, but it would be soon. The search would be called off about now. Not much chance of my being found today. I listened to the water lap against the boat. Frogs croaked and an owl hooted.

The hooting brought me straight up. I saw a light bumping up and down through the trees. A flashlight, I decided. My heart hammered as I caught sight of the figure behind it. He was coming this way. I ducked back into the boat and held back a scream, hoping whoever it was wouldn't see me.

My prayers came too late. The guy with the flashlight had seen me and was running toward the boat. I ducked farther down, but he shined the light on my face.

"Jessie?"

I relaxed a little. He knew my name and the voice sounded familiar. "Cooper," I guessed. "What are you doing here? Where are the others? Did the search-and-rescue team come?"

He lowered the flashlight then. "What are you babbling about? Why would I need rescuing?"

"Not you. Me. I got caught in the wind last night and ended up here. I'm stranded."

"Oh." He took another step toward me. "No kidding."

"Well, for once, Cooper, I'm really glad to see you. Where's your boat?"

He shook his head, apparently still trying to figure out why I was there. "I don't have a boat."

"Then how did you get here? I know you didn't swim."

"My grandpa brought me out. I have a camp—somewhere."

"You're camped here on the island, but you don't know where?"

He sighed. "Okay, I got lost. I got bored and decided to walk around the island, but you can't walk all the way around. There are some cliffs. Anyway, I came inland and got lost."

"Wow." I wasn't sure what to think. "Your grandfather just left you out here? Alone?"

"Yeah, alone. I've been watching *Survivor* and started learning all kinds of stuff about survival skills. I decided it was time to try out all the neat things I've learned."

"When is your grandfather coming back?"

"Sunday afternoon."

"But you could call him, right? And he could come and get you sooner?" I asked hopefully.

"Nope. He asked me if I wanted a cell phone, but I told him I didn't. I'm roughing it." He smiled as he said it.

"Could you row my boat back to Chenoa Lake?"

His face scrunched up. "Are you nuts? Do you have any idea how far that is?"

"I take it you can't?"

"No way. And even if I could, I wouldn't go out at night." Cooper folded his arms. "You're really stranded?"

"Unfortunately."

He licked his lips, deep in thought. For a minute I thought he might turn on me—do something really mean—but he didn't. "You look like you're cold. Don't you have a jacket?"

"N-no." I explained about the seagull.

Cooper scratched his head. "Bummer. They can get pretty aggressive. There's a few hanging around over at my camp—been bugging me all day. I got my food covered though. No way are they getting into my stuff." He hesitated. "I'd give you my sweatshirt, but I left it at camp."

"Um—do you have any idea where your camp is?" I asked.

"Sort of. I think it's on the other side of those rocks, maybe half a mile from here."

"You have to go through the woods?"

He nodded. "I came out here to this clearing, thinking I'd found it, but . . ." He shook his head. "I know it can't be very far. Do you want to come with me? I have an extra jacket and some food. You look like you could use something to eat."

"Thanks, but I'd better stay here with the boat." I sighed. "Besides, I can't walk very far right now."

"Okay." His gaze traveled to my bald head. "I might have a hat too."

"That would be nice."

"Tell you what. You wait here. I'll go back to my camp and get some food and a jacket. I'll be back as soon as I can."

"Thanks. I'll be here."

I watched him until the woods swallowed him up, hoping he'd make it back to his camp. I was worried, but figured the island wasn't all that big and that eventually he'd get there.

The dark stillness settled around me again, and I wished Cooper hadn't gone. Max would laugh when I told her how nice Cooper had been and how I actually missed him. I wasn't sure how long I'd sat there waiting for Cooper, but it seemed like at least an hour. I could hardly keep my eyes open, so I crawled back into the boat and settled down between the life jackets. Again, the frogs and crickets entertained me. Water lapped on the boat and gently rocked it.

Sometime later, another noise broke the serenity. Behind the chirping and bullfrogs croaking, I heard a steady *thump, thump, thump*. The thumping grew louder. I opened my eyes and saw a bright beam of light coming from the sky. At first I thought maybe I had died and that God was sending an angel down to get me. Then I realized it was a helicopter with a searchlight.

I couldn't see the helicopter itself; the light was too bright. But nothing made that sound or stirred up the air like a chopper.

I waved and stepped out of the boat. I thought it strange that the search-and-rescue teams would go up at night, but I let the thought slide, happy that I wouldn't have to spend the rest of the night alone.

The chopper swung away from me, and I thought they were going to leave me behind. The huge machine rose, then came down again, almost resting on the rocky point near where I'd been sitting most of the day. In the chopper's light I could see something drop to the ground. I started running toward it.

As quickly as it had come, the helicopter rose again and *thump, thump, thump*ed away. The searchlight was no longer on. They hadn't seen me or the boat.

"Wait! Wait for me!" I yelled. Hadn't they seen me? Then I realized that the light had never actually shined on me or the boat, only on the rocks and the trees.

I dropped onto my knees and started to cry. "Come back. Please come back."

CHAPTER EIGHTEEN

The helicopter had dropped a package. Maybe they'd seen me after all, and it was too dangerous to land so they left me a care package. The image of food and warm clothes propelled me toward the rocks. I stumbled, but managed to catch myself. When I reached the package, I tore into it, or tried to. The package had been wrapped in black plastic and tied in about ten places. I sat back, wishing I had something sharp and wondering why anyone would make a care package so hard to get into.

Maybe so it wouldn't scatter all over the place when they dropped it.

Or maybe it isn't food and clothes. Maybe it's drugs. I pushed the second possibility from my mind, determined to check out the contents. Working at a square of plastic, I managed to tear away some of the plastic. My fingers and arms hurt, but I couldn't stop. Under the black plastic was another layer. In the scant moonlight I could see a patch of white. I dug into it and felt something powdery. Something told me it wasn't dry milk.

As reality hit, I brushed the stuff from my fingers and backed away like I'd been stung. Drugs. The guy wasn't coming to rescue me at all. The island was being used as a drug drop. This meant only one thing. Someone would be coming to pick up the package, and he'd probably do it while it was still dark.

I folded the torn plastic back in as best I could and hurried back to my boat. Anyone coming for the package would see me, and I knew I should move the boat, but I couldn't. I had to rest and wait for Cooper. And try to stay alive for the rest of the night.

I lay back down but couldn't sleep. I kept thinking about the helicopter and the package I'd seen fall out of it. I hoped whoever planned to make the pickup would wait until morning. The sky had grown completely black, and the air smelled moist like it does before a heavy rain. "Not rain, please, God," I pleaded aloud. "No rain."

"Cooper, where are you?" I listened intently and peered into the woods for signs of his flashlight. *Where are you? Why haven't you come back?* Several answers swirled in my head. Cooper hadn't found his camp. Maybe he was hurt. Maybe Cooper had just decided to be a jerk and not come back. Or maybe the helicopter pilot had seen him.

I must have slept some during the night, though I have no idea how I managed it. I awoke as the sun came up. I was cold, but not wet. Shivering, I got out of the boat and jumped up and down to get my blood circulating. The life jackets had worked pretty well to insulate me.

I could see the package the helicopter had dropped the night before. The bundle was rectangular, about two feet wide and three long and about two feet deep. It was wrapped in black plastic and secured with duct tape.

I dropped onto the sand and thought about Cooper. Why hadn't he come back? Could he somehow be involved with drugs? Was that the real reason he'd come to the island? Was he really alone?

Somehow, I couldn't picture Cooper as a drug dealer. I had no reason not to believe him. But could I really trust my instincts? Then I wondered if he'd seen the helicopter and wondered again if he might be in danger. Maybe that was why he hadn't come back. Maybe whoever had come for the drugs had seen his camp and done something to him.

For the first time since I got to the island, I prayed that no one would come—at least not the people who were going to pick up the drugs. I tipped my head back and sighed. If drug dealers were coming I didn't want them to find me here. I needed to be out of sight and leave no trace that I had been here. I didn't know how much time I had, but I would have to get my boat and myself out of sight. Maybe I'd watched too much television, but I had a feeling if the people the package was meant for showed up and found me, they wouldn't be too thrilled. With the information I had, they'd probably have to kill me.

The sun was bright and hot by the time I managed to pull the boat up the sandy beach and into a stand of fir trees and vine maple. I'd set the vests back in the box to hide them from view. With the spring foliage out, the vine maple made a good shield for me to hide behind. When I'd finished hiding the boat, I was hot and sweaty and hungry and didn't want to do anything but sleep. I stumbled back to the lake to refill my water bottle. After drinking nearly all of it, I refilled it again and then went back to the boat to wait. I sat on a log at the forest's edge and listened for the sound of a motor boat or for voices.

I thought about hiking into the woods in an attempt to find Cooper, but decided against it. I was just too weak. I heard the sound of a plane and moved back into the brush. It flew overhead and I realized too late that it was probably one of the search-and-rescue planes. I should have been out there waving my arms. I should have had the orange life vests out there.

I wasn't thinking clearly. The person or persons coming to pick up the drugs were probably coming by boat. "Okay, Jessie," I mumbled to myself. "Next time you hear a plane or helicopter you are going to run out into the opening and wave your arms like crazy."

Waiting is the hardest thing in the world, especially when you can't do anything but think and worry. By noon I began to doubt that anyone would come. Maybe the drug pickup person would wait until dark. That would mean another night alone.

Or maybe not alone. I shivered. *What if the person picking up the drugs is here on the island right now? Maybe they live here or are camped out. What if Cooper had run into them or found their camp?* I got up and went back to the rock to look at the package in question.

Maybe you're wrong. Maybe it isn't drugs. But I knew it was. I pried out the loose plastic and watched a tiny stream of the powdery white substance slither to the ground. Another thought snared me. My fingerprints were on the package. I tucked the plastic back, securing it as best I could with the duct tape, then wiped the places I might have touched with my shirt.

Heading back to my boat, I heard a small engine. I ducked behind the brush and hoped no one could see my pink shirt. Relief spilled itself over and through me. Only one person sat in the boat that motored into the cove. Max.

I started to get up and held back. How could Max know I'd be here? Was Max coming for the package? Had Bob and Serena forced her to work for them? Max looked around the cove and started back out again. She wasn't there for the package. She was looking for me.

I jumped out from my hiding place. "Max! Wait!" I waved my arms as crazily as the seagull had flapped its wings. "Max!" I screamed, hoping she could hear me over the small motor. She glanced back at me and turned the boat around with such force, I thought she was going to sink it.

"Jessie!" she yelled back and waved.

I ran down to meet her. When she stepped out of the boat, I threw my arms around her.

She hugged me back. "What are you doing out here? Where's your boat? Man, I thought you'd gone over the falls. That's where I was looking this morning."

She moved back and grabbed my arms, her hands nearly circling my bony forearms. "Why did you take the boat out by yourself? What were you thinking?"

"Max. We don't have time to talk now. Please. We have to get your boat out of sight."

"What?" She let her arms drop to her sides. "You're delirious." She glanced around. "Where is your boat?"

I explained the situation the best I could while I tried to pull her boat out of the water. It was made of wood and far too heavy for me to handle alone.

"No kidding." She glanced up at the package, and I knew she had every intention of opening it.

"Please, Max," I grunted. "Help me hide the boat. It's too heavy for me."

Fortunately, she did as I asked.

We took off the motor to make the boat lighter. Once we'd hidden her boat, she pulled off her life jacket and shoved it, along with the motor, under the seat. When she straightened, she was holding a package of chips. "You must be hungry. Didn't you bring food?"

I told her about the seagull and she practically rolled on the ground laughing.

"It wasn't funny. I had to spend the night under a life jacket." I needed to tell her about Cooper too, but that could wait. I half expected him to show up anytime.

"I'm sorry. I have more food if you need it." She frowned. "You really think there are drugs in that package?"

"I'm sure. It's white and powdery. What else could it be? The pilot makes a drop at night. It's all wrapped up in black plastic. No one has come to get it yet." That's when I told her about Cooper.

Her eyes narrowed into tiny slits. "Cooper is here?"

I nodded. "He was. Unless I was dreaming. I guess that's possible."

"You must have been, kid, because there's no way Cooper Smally would be camping out here alone. I'm going to open the package."

"Please don't, Max. We don't want to get our prints on it. You'll just have to take my word for it."

"You have a point." She bit into a chip and offered me the bag.

I took a handful, and for the next few minutes I fed my face. I loved the salty taste on my tongue and the way they melted in my mouth. Mom never lets me eat chips at home. Too greasy and they're fried in a type of grease that turns toxic at high levels of heat. I felt guilty about eating them, but figured a few wouldn't hurt me. I felt even guiltier about something else—spying on Bob and Serena without telling Max.

I knew my parents had called her—told her I'd left a message saying I'd be at her place. Like she'd been reading my mind, she asked, "So why did you tell your parents you were with me?"

I shrugged, not knowing what to say.

"You should have told me." Max turned away from me, her gaze scanning the inlet.

"About what?"

"Quit playing games. I saw you, Jess. I saw you hanging around our back door."

I sucked in a sharp breath. "You saw me?"

"You went behind my back."

"I didn't want you to be mad at me and I . . ."

She pushed herself away from the log and took a step toward the water, then swung around. Arms folded and legs apart, she looked ready for a fight. "You were spying on Bob and Serena. Were you going to turn them in?"

I winced at the accusing tone in her voice. "I had to do something. You can't stay with them. I'm afraid they'll kill you or that you'll start using or . . ."

"I won't do drugs. I'm not stupid." She unfolded her arms and sat back down beside me. "They'd never kill me."

"They might. When people use cocaine they can get really weird. Remember when Mrs. Downing talked about the drug-induced rage in health?"

"They don't get that bad," she insisted again.

"Come on, Max, you don't have to be afraid of living with someone else. Being in foster care can be a good thing."

"Humph. A lot you know."

"I know you'd be a lot better off. Just because you had one bad experience . . ."

Max clamped her mouth shut and stared straight ahead. I knew there was no point in talking to her about it.

"Well," I said, "you really can't blame me. You come over and tell me we can't be friends anymore and that you're leaving. I don't want you to go. I thought if I could get some proof that Bob and Serena were into drugs, the police could arrest them and you'd be safe."

Max twisted around to look at me. "Did you get it? The proof, I mean?"

"I got a picture of Cody's car and wrote down the license plate. I heard them talking. I saw the briefcase full of money. I'm pretty sure that Cody was one of the guys arrested at the warehouse."

"So you're going to turn them in?"

"The seagull dropped my bag in the water, remember? My camera, my binoculars, and even my notepad were in it. All I have is what I saw, and the police may not even believe me—especially after the fiasco at the gift shop."

"Shh. I hear something."

I heard it too. We ducked into the brush as the small fishing boat *putt-putt*ed into the cove and headed straight for the sandy beach. My chest tightened. I could hardly breathe. "Max, look. It's the guy from the store."

Danny Edwards glanced around as he pulled the boat onto shore.

He scanned the tree line. Apparently satisfied that he wasn't being watched, he climbed up onto the rock. Without opening the package, he lifted it onto his shoulder and carried it back to his boat. He was in and out of there in less than five minutes.

Max narrowed her eyes again, and I thought for a minute she was going to go after him. "He's getting away. I could tackle him and . . ."

I put a restraining hand on her arm. "Let him go. When we're sure he's gone, we can go to the police. Detective Johnson will check it out—especially when I tell him about the helicopter. Besides, the guy might have a gun."

When he'd cleared the cove, Max and I started dragging her rental boat and my rowboat down to the water. She did most of the dragging; I could barely walk. Since I was too weak to row, she tied the prow of my boat onto the back of hers.

"What about Cooper?" I asked. "What if he's really camped here? He seemed nice and . . ."

"Which proves it had to be a dream."

"I don't think so. I'm afraid something might have happened to him."

"If we don't want that guy getting away with those drugs, we have to get out into the open water where the search teams can spot us."

We didn't have to wait long. Once we cleared the island and were about 100 yards out in open water, a plane flew overhead and Max and I waved. Within minutes Sheriff Clark showed up on the sheriff's boat. They circled us and closed in. My dad was on board, leaning out so far to reach for me, I thought he would fall in.

"Jessie, Max. Thank God you're safe." Dad had tears in his eyes and used his shirt sleeve to brush them away.

I thought I was in for a huge lecture, but he took one look at me and yelled at the sheriff, "We need to get her on board now. Call 911. Have the paramedics meet us at the dock in town."

"I must look pretty bad, huh?" I asked Max. All the while she'd been rowing, I'd been lying down, feeling too weak to sit.

She didn't answer, but I took her silence as a yes.

My dad and the sheriff fished me out of Max's rental boat and wrapped me in blankets. Dad carried me below deck and settled me on one of the bunks. "Stay here. I'll be right back."

Going somewhere was the last thing on my mind.

The next thing I knew, Max was in the cabin with me. Dad thanked her for finding me. "I just wish you'd told us where you were going, Max," he said.

"I didn't think anyone really cared." Max ducked her head.

"They do, Max. We do." After checking me over again, he asked, "How did you know where to look for her?"

Max tossed me a worried look. "I knew she wouldn't be able to row very far. Coming down the lake wasn't a problem because she had the current and the wind behind her. But I knew going back, she'd have a tough time, especially with the wind coming off the mountain. Yesterday after you called me, I headed for the falls. See, I figured if she got caught in the current that's where she'd end up. When that didn't pan out I went to the beach access by my place and did a little calculating. I figured she had to have been blown toward the other side of the lake. And since there was no sign of her on the lake itself, the next logical step was that she'd ended up on one of the islands."

"So you've been out looking for her since yesterday morning."

Max nodded. "Except for going home to sleep."

"Why didn't you tell us what you were thinking? We wasted a lot of time searching the upper end of the lake."

"I didn't think anyone would listen to me." Max chewed on her lower lip. "When you called I wasn't completely honest with you. I thought maybe Jessie was hiding out or something. She wasn't at my place, but what I didn't tell you was that she had been there around one in the morning."

He frowned and turned toward me. "Jessie, why would you sneak out like that? If you wanted to stay at Max's, you could have asked."

"She didn't come to stay overnight, Mr. Miller." Max took a deep breath. "Jessie was trying to save me."

"We got the boats in tow, Mr. Miller," the sheriff said as he leaned down from the top of the stairs. "You folks need anything?"

"No," Dad said. "Just get us back to town as fast as you can." The engine powered up, and we were under way.

"Sheriff, wait," I called up to him. I sounded weak and felt even weaker. "There's something I need to tell you, and it's really important."

"All right." Sheriff Clark frowned and lowered himself onto the bunk next to me.

I told him about the helicopter and the bundle the pilot had dropped on the island.

"This guy came and got it not more than an hour ago," Max said. "You'll never guess who picked it up."

"Are you going to tell me?" he asked.

"Danny Edwards, who happens to work at a gift shop where I told Detective Johnson to go a few weeks ago. I knew he was into drugs."

"I see. And you think this package contains drugs?"

"Yes," I said. "I looked. Anyway, I don't know what else it could be—I mean who else would drop a package on a deserted island at night?"

"Makes sense to me, Jessie," he finally said. "I'll get on the horn right now. With any luck we can catch Mr. Edwards before he gets rid of this mystery package."

"Um, Sheriff," I said. "Maybe you should just keep an eye on him—see who he distributes to and . . ." I told him about Bob and Serena and what I had witnessed the night before last.

The sheriff shook his head. "As much as I appreciate the information, this is a matter for the authorities, not for a couple kids."

"Is this true, Max?" Dad asked. "Are your aunt and uncle dealing and using drugs?"

Max stared at her hands, which she'd folded on her lap. "I thought if their supply dried up, they'd stop using. I didn't know they were dealing too."

She looked up at the sheriff. "Are you going to arrest me?"

Sheriff Clark placed a hand on her shoulder. "Were you in any way involved?"

Head down again, she nodded. "I took money sometimes. I guess I knew they were dealing. I just didn't want to admit it. I don't want anything bad to happen to them."

"Max." Sheriff Clark knelt down in front of her. "This isn't your fault, and you shouldn't have to suffer because of their bad judgment. Your aunt and uncle will be better off in a facility where they can get help to end their drug use and hopefully rehabilitate. You'll have to come down to the station and tell us what you know."

"Max, I had no idea things were this bad for you," Dad said. "If it's all right with CPS, we'll have you stay with us for a while. That is, if you want to."

"Thanks, Dad. Do it, Max," I said. Turning to the sheriff, I added, "There's one more thing." I told him about seeing Cooper on the island. "He said he was coming back to bring me food and stuff, but he never did. I'm worried he might be hurt or something."

"You say his grandfather dropped him off on the island alone?"

I nodded. My eyes were so heavy, I had to close them. Max and the sheriff sounded far away, like they were in some kind of tunnel.

"Jessie?" I heard my name, but couldn't speak. I wondered for a minute if I might be dying. Then I couldn't hear anymore.

CHAPTER TWENTY

When I woke up I was in the hospital with a needle in my arm and two different fluids dripping into the tube. Guess I hadn't died after all. Mom was sitting next to me, resting her head and arms on my bed. "Mom?"

She lifted her head and smiled at me. "Hey, sleepyhead, I wondered when you'd wake up."

"What happened?" I yawned.

"You fainted on the boat."

"Where's Max?"

"In school." Mom straightened the covers over me. "She'll be here soon."

"Am I in trouble?"

"Yes, but we'll talk about that later. We'll probably have to ground you."

"Do I get to count the time I'm here?"

Mom smiled. "Oh, Jessie, what am I going to do with you?"

I remembered what Dad had said about Max staying with us.

"Is Max okay? Did the sheriff find the package? Did they arrest Bob and Serena and Cody and . . ."

"Slow down, sweetie. There's plenty of time for all that. I need to let the nurse know you're awake."

"Why?"

She stroked my forehead and kissed me. "You've been asleep for two days. We've been very worried."

I felt pretty good, which meant I'd probably gotten blood. I couldn't believe I'd been asleep so long. "Is Max okay?"

"She's fine. And yes, she's staying with us until CPS can find her a suitable home."

"Why can't she stay with us forever? You should keep her, Mom, and then when I die, you'll still have a daughter and Sam will have a sister."

"Jessie . . ." Sudden tears moistened her eyes.

"I'm sorry. I didn't mean to make you cry."

She took a tissue out of the box on my bedside table and dabbed at the wetness on her cheeks. After a while she said, "You'll be okay. In fact, you're going to be fine. We have a donor for you."

"Right. So when do I get the bone marrow?"

"As soon as you're strong enough. Maybe as early as next week."

Mom left and came back. The nurse checked me over and took my vital signs—pulse, blood pressure, temperature, and oxygen levels. I wondered how I'd managed to sleep two days. Most of the time when I'm in the hospital I'm awake every two hours at least.

After the nurse left, Mom and I talked for a while longer about family stuff and how they'd moved Max into my room. "Your bedroom is a bit crowded," Mom said, "but I'm sure you'll manage."

I smiled. "I'll love having Max for a roommate."

Mom laughed. "I'm sure you will."

You'd think after sleeping for so long, I'd be awake for days, but my eyelids kept closing and Mom told me to rest. She picked up the novel she'd been reading and settled back into the chair.

The next time I woke up, Mom was gone and Cooper Smally was standing next to my bed.

"Hey," he said.

"Cooper!" I felt like hugging him. "What happened to you? Why didn't you come back?"

He pressed his lips together and lifted his arm. "Guess." He had a cast on his left arm.

"I was right, you did get hurt. What happened?"

"My flashlight went out and I got scared. I couldn't see anything. I heard this growl and thought it was a bear. I tried to climb up a tree—only I couldn't hold on. I fell and landed on my arm."

"I'm sorry." I tipped my head to the side. "Was it a bear?"

"I have no idea. Guess the noise scared it away." He sighed. "Anyway, I'm the one who should be sorry. It was morning before I made it back to my camp. I hurt so bad, I couldn't do anything but lie there."

"It's okay, Cooper. You tried."

"Thanks for telling the sheriff about me. They told me they

rescued you and Max. The sheriff told me about the drug drop. I heard the helicopter too."

I checked out his cast. "Does it hurt much?"

"Not anymore." He glanced down at the floor. "I wanted to tell you something else too. I haven't been very nice to you, and I'm sorry."

"It's okay."

He moved his head from side to side. "No, it isn't. I've been doing a lot of thinking lately."

"Consider yourself forgiven." I smiled. "How come you're not in school?"

"It's out." The answer came from Max, not Cooper. Max came in and stood on the opposite side of the bed. "Nice of you to apologize, Cooper." She gave him a knowing grin, and I had no doubt that she'd talked to him.

"Did you two come here together?"

"Maybe," Max said. "We might have ridden our bikes in the same direction."

She didn't need to tell me. Somewhere along the way, she and Cooper had become friends, and as impossible as that sounded, it felt right.

"So what happened with the drug bust?" I asked. "Did they catch Danny Edwards? Did they arrest Bob and Serena?"

"For such a little kid, you sure ask a lot of questions." Max grinned. "Yeah, they caught Edwards. And it turns out I was right about the gift shop. Edwards had an operation at his house. He'd put packages of cocaine into vases and bring them to the store to sell them to Bob and some other suppliers. Detective Johnson said to thank you. This was their biggest bust yet, and for now, at least, Chenoa Lake is drug free."

"That's great. What about Bob and Serena?" I asked. "Are they in jail?"

Max tipped her head. "They were arrested. I think they'll be in jail for a long time. I feel kind of bummed about it, but like your dad says, maybe now they'll get the help they need. You were right, Jess. It was stupid of me to think I could help them by cutting off their supply."

"I'm sorry."

"Don't be." Max brightened. "I'll survive."

I knew she would. I looked from Max to Cooper, thankful to have them as friends. Things were definitely looking up.

"Hey, we brought you something." Max held up a white bag from the tea shop.

"Thanks." I took it from her and opened it. Inside the bag was a box containing six perfect chocolate-dipped strawberries. I inhaled the sweet fragrance and set them on the bedside table. "You have to help me eat them." Max and Cooper practically swallowed theirs whole. I took my time savoring the luscious sweet fruit and the delicious chocolate. I hope God has chocolate-dipped strawberries in heaven.

ACKNOWLEDGMENTS

Thanks to Marilyn, Elsie, Maria, Birdie, and Marion for their encouragement and support.

For Lauraine, who never stopped believing in Max & Me.

For my agents, Chip McGregor and Andy McGuire, for getting Max & Me into print and out to my favorite fans.

ABOUT THE AUTHOR

Internationally known author and speaker **Patricia H. Rushford** has book sales totaling over a million copies. She has written numerous articles and authored over forty books, including *What Kids Need Most in a Mom, Have You Hugged Your Teenager Today?*, and *It Shouldn't Hurt to be a Kid*. She also writes a number of mystery series: *The Jennie McGrady Mysteries* for kids and the *Helen Bradley Mysteries* for adults. Her latest releases include: *The McAllister Files, She Who Watches, The Angel Delaney Mysteries* with *As Good as Dead* and a romantic suspense, *Sins of the Mother*. Her newest series for children is *The Max & Me Mysteries*.

One of her mysteries, *Silent Witness,* was nominated for an Edgar by Mystery Writers of America and won the Silver Angel for excellence in media. *Betrayed* was selected as best mystery for young adults *The Oregonian* (1997) and won the Phantom Friends Award. *Morningsong,* a romantic suspense, won the Golden Quill for Inspirational Romance award.

Patricia is a registered nurse and holds a Master's Degree in Counseling. In addition, she conducts writers workshops for adults and children and is codirector of *Writer's Weekend at the Beach*. She is the current director of the Oregon Christian Writers Summer Conference. Pat has appeared on numerous radio and television talk shows across the U.S. and Canada. She lives in the Portland, Oregon, area with her husband.

www.patriciarushford.com
Author/Speaker
What Kids Need Most in a Mom
The Jennie Mcgrady Mysteries
The McAllister Files
The Angel Delaney Mysteries
The Helen Bradley Mysteries
The Max & Me Mysteries (New!)